THE BOY
WHO DIDN'T
WANT TO
DIE

PETER LANTOS

THE BOY WHO DIDN'T WANT TO DIE

SCHOLASTIC

Published in the UK by Scholastic, 2023

1 London Bridge, London, SE1 9BG
Scholastic Ireland, 89E Lagan Road,
Dublin Industrial Estate,
Glasnevin, Dublin, D11 HP5F

ISBN 978 07023 2308 9

A CIP catalogue record for this book
is available from the British Library.

Printed by CPI Group (UK) Ltd, Croydon, CR0 4YY

Papers used by Scholastic Children's Books are made
from wood grown in sustainable forests.

1 3 5 7 9 10 8 6 4 2

www.scholastic.co.uk

To the memory of my mother ...
and to all the children who perished in the Holocaust

Contents

1. The journey begins   1

2. In the ghetto   19

3. Leaving Hungary   33

4. In the Vienna Woods   50

5. Arriving in Bergen-Belsen   62

6. Surviving in a concentration camp   76

7. Destination unknown   99

8. The first days of freedom   110

9. Escape from the Russians   128

10. Shock in Budapest   138

11. Homecoming   148

12. My first day at school   170

    You may want to know...

    What happened next   175

    About the places on my journey   193

    Glossary   207

    Acknowledgments   215

Chapter 1

The journey begins

On a sunny March afternoon in 1944, I did not know that my life was going to be turned upside down within the next couple of months. I was walking through our timber yard, holding my mum's hand. I wasn't even five yet, but keeping my eyes and ears open, I knew that there had been warning signs that things might change. Until recently, I'd felt safe here, since this was my world. Everything I could see around me belonged to us. We were going home from my uncle Sándor's and aunt Anna's villa, where I often played with my cousin Zsuzsi, who was my age. We always got on well. She didn't even cry when I took away her toys. We used to have the same governess, Maria, who was paid by my uncle because my dad didn't have enough money. Then one day Maria stopped coming to take care of us. My mother explained that Aunt Anna could not employ her any longer.

When I asked why, Mum said it was because we were Jewish. She said no more, and I didn't understand why us being Jewish would mean Maria had to leave.

My uncle didn't actually live in the villa anymore. I'd once asked where he was, and Aunt Anna answered that he had been called up to do hard labour on the eastern front in Russia. To stop me asking further questions, Aunt Anna explained that Jewish men could not be regular soldiers, but they were needed to do heavy work on the front, like digging trenches to protect the soldiers. He had gone away a long time ago, and we had not heard from him since. This was the first time I realized that a war was going on, and my country, Hungary, was fighting on Germany's side.

Earlier, I had spent the day playing with Zsuzsi as usual. She was very pretty, with long dark hair and large brown eyes. These she must have inherited from her mother, who was also very beautiful. Aunt Anna had prepared a lovely lunch but apologized that she hadn't been able to get the food she wanted. There was no meat, only *krumpli paprikás* – a dish of sliced potatoes with lots of ground red pepper. My mum called this the "poor man's stew", but it tasted good! Afterwards we were treated to Aunt Anna's stewed quince compote made from the fruit that had been saved over the winter. After lunch, my mother had picked me up to take me home.

Now we were walking through our timber yard, which seemed immense in the dusk of early spring – so large that I could not see its borders, which were marked by a fence. Facing the main street, on either side of the small office building, stood the two villas belonging to my uncles. Next to the bottom of the yard was our more modest house.

In the centre of the yard was the star attraction: an enormous shed which housed the electric saws. I was told never to go in there, since they were dangerous. Of course, I knew this. Mum must have been frightened by the thought that, instead of logs, her son would be sawn into pieces.

From the shed a small-gauge track ran to the bottom of the yard. One side of the track was lined with large piles of logs, which were carried by carts to the electric saws to be cut. The finished products, planks of the same thickness, were deposited on the other side. The piled-up logs and planks were high enough for Zsuzsi and me to play hide-and-seek in. This was good fun but discouraged by our mothers.

The whole yard was dominated by a cooling tower, and I found its dark pool of water rather frightening. Next to it was the most exciting place: the engine room. It was Dad who took me there after my repeated requests and introduced me to a large man with a moustache who wore overalls. He told me that he was the engineer and tried to explain what the machines did. The machines moved tirelessly and noisily: I was fascinated. And there was a smell there like nowhere else. I thought it must have been the warm machine oil, drops of which had made the floor next to the machine slippery. Dad told me that the wood was bought by building firms, and it was a successful business.

Once, this yard had been filled with workers. Sometimes I would walk through the timber yard on my own and stop and talk with them or listen to their conversations. Their speech was rather different from my parents', and they used some words I didn't understand. I picked up expressions that my mother didn't like, saying that they were not very polite.

One day, this had led to big trouble.

Mum had invited a couple of her friends and Aunt Anna for morning coffee and cake. When I entered the living room and saw them sitting around drinking coffee, I used one of these words just to surprise them. And surprised they were.

Deadly silence followed. Everyone looked at me. I realized that I must have said something I shouldn't, but I didn't know what. Mum jumped up, apologized to her guests and, catching my hand, dragged me into my bedroom. She was angry. Very angry. I have never seen her so angry. She had hardly shut the door behind her before: "Where did you hear *that* word?"

"What word?" I wasn't sure what she was talking about.

"The word you just said. Do you know what it means?" I thought it was better to remain silent, but my mother did not give up.

"Where did you hear it?"

"I heard it in the timber yard. From the workers."

"You should never use that word again. Never. Promise."

I nodded my head in agreement and added, for emphasis, "I promise."

"Now come with me and apologize. Then I'll explain to the guests what happened."

I did as she said. When I told this story to Gyuri, my brother, in the evening, he could hardly hold in his laughter.

"What's so funny?"

"Never mind. What other words did you learn from the workers?"

I had quite a list.

"You seem to have quite a good collection of swear words. You should never use any of them. Mum is right, of course; these words are never used in polite society. When you grow up, you'll understand." I expected to hear more about these words and what polite society was, but he didn't say anything else.

The workers who had "taught" me this word were no longer around. The timber yard was now completely deserted. The machines were silent and only a caretaker was about. Dad had told me that the timber yard was not ours anymore and there would be different people running it. He'd also lost his job as an accountant.

As we arrived home, Dad asked my mum even before she could remove her coat: "Have you heard the news?"

"No. Should I have?"

"The Germans have invaded Hungary. The radio just announced it."

Mum gasped. "I can't believe it! We're their ally."

"If you don't believe it, we can listen to the BBC World Service later."

This is how all the bad things started. I didn't know it then, but within a couple of months, everything we had would be taken away. And that was not even the worst thing that would happen to us.

At the time, I was too young really to understand what was going on outside of my own life, but dramatic events had been unfolding across Europe. We were in the middle of a war. My dad explained that it was a world war. When I asked him what a world war was, instead of answering, he removed a large book from the bookshelf and opened it.

"This is called an atlas: it's a collection of maps of the countries around the world." He opened it and outlined an odd-shaped blob: "This is Hungary." He then pointed near the top of the blob. "This is Budapest, and this," he said, dragging his finger further down, "is Makó, where we live."

He turned the page. "This is Europe. Each coloured area is a country. For example, this is Germany and this is France. And this is part of the Soviet Union." He pointed at the red-coloured patch, the largest on the map. "The war began some time ago: in 1939, the year you were born. Germany occupied many countries in Europe, but fortunately not Great Britain."

"Why did Germany start the war?"

Dad hesitated for a moment. "They wanted more power, more territory and they wanted to get revenge for the previous war, which they had lost. And their leader, Adolf Hitler, is evil. He wants to murder all the Jews in Europe." I was not sure that I understood all this, but did not dare to ask more questions. Just as well, as Dad had turned the page.

"This is Asia. The war is being fought there." He turned to another page, showing an area which looked like an upside-down pear. "This is Africa, and the war is going on there too. That's why this war is called a world war – it's taking place all over the world."

Dad explained that, at the beginning, it looked like Germany, joined by Italy and Japan, would win. Now, however, the Allies – America, Great Britain and the Soviet Union – were more likely to be victorious. The war was in its fifth year and had finally reached us: the Germans had invaded our country.

My dad was shorter than my mum, but both were slim. I never knew the colour of my mum's eyes, since they always seemed to change in different lights: sometimes brown, then grey or green. Her hair was quite dark, practically black. She always looked smart, even at home, although her dresses were not as expensive as Aunt Anna's.

Dad didn't have much hair, and the top of his head was completely bald. I don't remember the colour of his eyes, but when he was angry – which was not often – I didn't like to look into them.

When I was a little younger, I asked Gyuri how old our parents were. He told me that Mum was over forty and Dad was even older. I couldn't believe it, so I asked our mother. She confirmed what Gyuri had told me. Being over forty seemed a terribly old age. I told her that Aunt Anna was much younger, to which she answered: "Your aunt doesn't have a son of eighteen, does she?" This was true, I had to admit. Dad being even older worried me; they might die before having time to bring me up.

I had learned early on, partly from keeping my eyes open and partly from overhearing my parents' occasional arguments, that we were the poorest in Mum's large family of five brothers and three sisters. It was again Gyuri who explained that Dad, as an accountant, did not earn much. To help us out, Grandma occasionally lent us some money.

Our house was modest in size, much smaller than Zsuzsi's, and had only two bedrooms. There was also a large living room, a bathroom and a kitchen: that was all. We had a small garden at the back, surrounded by a wooden fence from which a gate led straight to the timber yard.

I shared my bedroom with Gyuri. He was fourteen years older than me and not a child anymore. When he undressed, I could see that he had hair over his body: on his legs, between his legs and under his arms. I hoped I was going to be like him when I grew up. He was tall, or anyway he seemed tall to me; he had brown wavy hair and deeply set brown eyes. He wore glasses, and I thought that reading so much must have weakened his sight. I couldn't imagine him without a book.

We got on well with the unspoken rule that he bore my

boisterous presence with patience. Whenever I interrupted his reading, he answered my questions as if he had all the time in the world and in a way that meant I could understand his explanations. He was shy, and when I asked him whether he had a girlfriend, he pretended not to hear me, but he blushed. I didn't ask a second time, but I thought that he did.

Mum told me that Gyuri was very bright, and he finished the local high school with a baccalaureate with distinction: he got the highest marks in all subjects. I should follow his example, she said. Yet when he applied to the Faculty of Humanities (whatever they were) of the university, he was not admitted. My mother explained the reason was because he was Jewish. I realized at this early age that to be Jewish in Hungary was not a good thing.

It was soon after the Germans invaded the country that Gyuri was called up to do hard labour. He had to follow my uncle's example. My parents were very upset, particularly my mother. One time I caught her crying. Over the next couple of days, the house became very quiet and I didn't even feel like going to play with Zsuzsi.

Our mother helped Gyuri to prepare his luggage. It didn't take very long. Once the suitcase was ready, I saw Gyuri cramming a couple of books in under his shirts.

I remember the day of his departure. I was playing with one of my toys: a grey mouse which, when wound up, crisscrossed the table without ever falling off. As I was watching and putting small obstacles in its way, suddenly a hand lifted the mouse from its run before I could protest; it was Gyuri, who had come to say goodbye. He had already said farewell to my parents, who were standing behind him. I could see that Mum had been crying. He lifted me from the ground, held me in his arms, kissed me and said, "Be good."

And then he left.

It was so unexpected that I failed to say anything. We never saw him again.

On the first evening after Gyuri left, I realized that I had become sole master of the bedroom. Yet I missed his company very much. He had answered questions I was too scared to ask my parents. He occasionally read a couple of paragraphs from his books when I asked what he was reading and explained things to me. He gently woke me up in the mornings; now Mum had to do it. In the evenings there was nobody in the next bed, no one who would whisper to me in the dark when he came in late. "Are you awake? You should be asleep," he would say when he heard me moving, and come over to my bed to adjust the blanket.

Without him, I felt less protected. It was not the darkness of the bedroom that bothered me – I never felt afraid of the dark – but when I was woken in the middle of the night by a bad dream, his even breathing was reassuring.

It was then that I realized I loved him and regretted not telling him this before he left. When I asked Mum whether I could sleep in his bed, she said, "No," and I knew I shouldn't ask a second time.

I started to notice that our meals were not as good as they used to be. My mother explained that Hungary had been in the war for three years, and now, with the German invasion, some food had become scarce. In the past, we had often had chickens and ducks, occasionally a goose, but now even a chicken on our table was a rare thing.

Although our kitchen, unlike my grandparents', was not kosher, we never ate pork or bacon. I learned early that kosher meant not eating pork and shellfish, never mixing meat and milk, and many other rules as Jewish law ordered. More frequently, we were having dishes without meat. My favourite was pancakes filled with cottage cheese, which I liked even more than meat. I could have eaten dozens, particularly when my mum put raisins in the filling.

One morning I noticed her sitting by the living room window sewing. It was not often that she sewed, so I was curious to see what she was doing. I was surprised to see that, from a yellow velvety material, she was cutting out a large Star of David, a symbol of the Jewish community.

"What are you doing?"

"Can't you see?" she said, quite upset.

I didn't understand why I had upset her. "You're making Stars of David. But what for?"

"For us to wear." Seeing my confusion, she added, "There's a new law: Jews have to wear a Star of David."

"But why? We know we're Jewish."

"It's so that other people know we're Jewish."

"Do I have to wear one too?"

"No, you're too young."

"But I want to wear one."

"Don't be difficult; you can't wear one. Only children older than you can wear one."

"Will Zsuzsi have one?"

"Of course not. She's your age."

That settled the matter. If Zsuzsi wasn't going to wear one, perhaps I shouldn't.

It was only a few weeks later, in May, at a Friday night dinner at my grandparents' house, that I began to understand this was not the only thing that would change.

Their house was on one of the most beautiful streets in town, lined by two rows of lime and chestnut trees. The lime trees filled the air with a strong fragrance at the end of June, while the chestnut trees flowered much earlier, in May.

The house had more rooms than ours and more than even Uncle Sándor's villa. When all the interconnecting double doors were opened, we could race around, and this is exactly what Zsuzsi and I did after we arrived.

But the real attraction was the bathroom. The room itself was big, with a very large cast-iron bath and a gigantic water tank fixed in one corner of the ceiling. On the outside of the tank there was a marker, indicating how much water was inside. There was a hand pump attached, and when the water was getting low the handyman or one of the bigger boys was asked to pump water for the next bath.

In one corner stood the foreign miracle of the time: a water closet, which is basically the same as a toilet. This one was referred to as the English water closet, indicating the country of origin. My mother told me that when the house was finished, it had been the only one in town: no wonder people had wanted to see it.

Our race was interrupted by a voice which did not expect any contradiction.

"If you want to run around, go into the garden. This is *not* an athletics ground."

We immediately stopped in our tracks, but on this occasion we did not take up Grandma's offer. The garden had not recovered from winter and we didn't want to go out into the spring chill. We would have to wait for it to come fully alive.

The garden was large and consisted of two parts. At the front, immediately behind and at the side of the house there were flower beds, large ornamental box trees and lilac bushes. Separated from these was a fruit and vegetable garden, tended seasonally by a gardener.

The voice that had stopped us belonged to Grandma Fanny, and the idea of not obeying her at once didn't even cross our minds. Everybody obeyed Grandma Fanny without question. She was the head of the family. Since Grandpa Samuel's death, she had been running the household and she had control over the money. Grandpa had died so many years before that I knew him only from my mum's stories and from his oil portrait in the living room. When I asked why Grandpa had died, Mum explained that he'd had bleeding in the brain and could not move or speak.

Although Grandma Fanny was very much alive, her portrait also hung next to Grandpa's. It was like her in real life: pale skin and neatly brushed white hair, but it was her bluish-grey eyes that dominated her face. She was small, but her forceful character made up for her being short.

Later, she called us to dinner. I wanted to sit next to Zsuzsi, but Grandma's finger pointed to a chair between my parents.

A couple of years before, there would have been more family members, but on this Friday night, apart from us, Aunt Anna and Zsuzsi, only Uncle Jenő was there. He was my mother's youngest brother of five: a tall, lanky figure with a big nose and balding head. He was wearing a very nice new suit, which led Mum to comment, "Jenő, such a beautiful suit." Everybody laughed, including Grandma. I didn't understand why it was funny, until Mum explained later. Since there were five brothers in her family, clothes were always handed down the chain from the oldest to the youngest. It was always Uncle Jenő who got the most-worn suits. Although my grandparents could have afforded new suits for each of their children, Grandma's legendary thriftiness usually won the day. Anyway, the family's tailor always ordered the best material from England, which seemed to last for ever.

Grandma lit the candles and said the prayers: we were all expected to join her for the blessing of wine and bread. She prayed in Hebrew, as did the other adults. I could not read Hebrew yet; boys usually learned it before their Bar Mitzvah at the age of thirteen, unless you were a member of a very religious Orthodox family, which we were not.

Grandma asked my mum to help serve the food and they disappeared into the kitchen. The cook and the cleaner had stopped coming to help some time before. The food was a delicious chicken in the pot. The portions, when divided into seven, were small, but the noodles and vegetables made up for it. I couldn't complain, because I got a wing, which was my favourite.

After dinner, the conversation turned to a subject I did not understand. The word "ghetto" was repeated several times. I looked at Zsuzsi, who, catching my eye, shrugged her shoulders. She didn't know what the word meant either.

"What is a ghetto?" I asked. There was silence. My dad looked at my mum and in turn she looked at Grandma.

"Ili," Grandma turned towards my mother, "haven't you told Peter?" Mum shook her head.

"And you, Anna? Does Zsuzsi know?" Aunt Anna also shook her head.

"You should have told them," was Grandma's verdict.

I suddenly realized that whatever "ghetto" meant, it couldn't be a good thing. And perhaps I shouldn't have asked.

We left earlier than usual, maybe because there was no cake after the meal. As we were walking home from my grandparents' house, we didn't know that we were not going to have another Friday night family dinner for a very long time.

Chapter 2

In the ghetto

The next day being Saturday, as if nothing happened, we went to the synagogue.

I remembered the first occasion I'd gone to the synagogue with my parents, a year or so before. They had explained, before we left the house, that Jews were not all the same. There were the Orthodox Jews, who took every word of the Torah, the sacred book of the Jews, as it was written, while we were different, more modern. We were the "Neolog" Jews, and before I could ask my mother what that meant, she said: "It means that the practice of religion is newly interpreted to suit the modern age."

"But we do believe in the same God?"

"Yes, of course. At school, you'll learn all about it and much more."

We had a separate synagogue, newer and much larger

than the Orthodox one. In our synagogue they played music, and there was even a large organ which, at full blast, could raise the roof. My parents told me that Grandpa Samuel, who was a leading member of the Jewish community and a member of the town council, had donated quite a lot of money to get the synagogue built.

In the synagogue, my parents sat in different parts: I was with Dad on the ground floor with all the men, while Mum was in the balcony with the women. I always wanted to see where she was sitting and was happy when I recognized her hat or silver scarf.

However, this Saturday was rather different from the day of my first visit to the synagogue. As we headed back home from the synagogue after service, my mum said, "Now listen: we're going away."

I did not know why, but I felt that something terrible was going to happen. My world was coming to an end. Everything was going to disappear: our homes, the timber yard, my uncles' villas, my grandparents' house… What was I going to do? I wanted to cry but thought the better of it, and we went inside the house. I wanted to know more.

"On holiday?" I asked hopefully, although I knew that it was not summer yet, which is when we usually went away.

"No, it is *not* a holiday."

"Where are we going then?"

"Not very far. We're just moving to another part of town."

"But why?"

"We have to. We have no choice. It's an order."

"Who ordered it?"

My dad, who had been silent, answered, "The mayor, instructed by the government."

Suddenly I remembered the talk at the end of last night's dinner. "What's the place called?"

"It's called a ghetto." My mother explained that, a long time ago, Jews were not allowed to settle in just any part of the town they liked, but were restricted to certain areas, called ghettos. Now, all Jews in the town and all over the country were ordered by law to leave their homes.

"But lots of Jews live in two streets in the centre of town anyway, in Small Jewish Street and Great Jewish Street. Were they forced to live there?"

"They weren't. It just happened. Those streets were close to the market, and they thought that they would be safer if they lived in the same area. Later, the synagogues were built there."

"But no one from our family lives in that area. Why not?"

"Your grandparents wanted to be part of the whole town, not just the Jewish community."

I wasn't quite sure what she meant, but she continued:

"When your grandparents bought and extended the timber yard, they built the two villas and our house next to it. And all this is far from the Jewish streets."

"But now we have to leave our house to go to the ghetto. Why?" I pressed. "We haven't done anything wrong."

"No, we haven't, but we are Jewish and that's bad enough."

"What's wrong with being Jewish?" I asked.

"There's nothing wrong with being Jewish. But the Hungarian government and the Germans think that Jews have harmed their countries, and this is a sort of punishment."

"How long are we going to stay in the ghetto?"

"I don't know. But I do know that if you keep asking me questions and holding me up, I can't finish the list of things we can take with us."

At this point I thought it was better to stop questioning and changed tack. "Can I help?" I asked.

"No, you can't," Mum replied, but after a second, she changed her mind. "Yes, you can. You can help to prepare our luggage."

It was at that moment that I realized we really were going to leave the house where I had been born and where we had always lived.

"What can we take with us?" I asked. Then, having sized up

the suitcases lined up on the floor of the living room, I added, "This luggage isn't large enough to take all our clothes."

"Of course not. Tomorrow we will send the furniture we can take: one bed, one chair, and a blanket and one mattress – between us. Your dad is in charge of that. You can help me with the rest. There is a list which tells us how many pieces we can take. It isn't much. Two coats, two changes of clothes, two pairs of shoes and four changes of underwear. You can help me to pack the suitcases."

"Can I take my toys?"

"I'm afraid you can't. There just isn't enough space."

Preparing our luggage took a long time and Mum kept changing her mind about which pieces of clothing we might need. Seeing her putting my winter coat into one of the suitcases, I asked, "Are we staying in the ghetto for the winter?"

"I don't know, but it might come in useful."

A couple of days later, two officials, accompanied by a man in a uniform, came to our house. His uniform was different from a police officer's, and it seemed more military, like a soldier's. But what caught my eye was his helmet, decorated with what looked like a cockerel's feather. Dad later explained that he was not a regular policeman but one of the gendarmes. They were a different force, and their job was to maintain law and order in the service of the government.

The gendarme was not very friendly. The officials asked my parents to tell them what we had left behind and checked that we had not packed anything that we should not have. They asked questions more than once about money and jewellery and threatened that they would search the place if we lied. My parents confirmed that they had given everything to the people who ordered them to do so.

It was towards the end of May when we left our house. My mother cried and Dad tried to console her. I nearly joined her, but with the firm knowledge that I had my toy mouse in my pocket, I felt strong and brave.

Arriving in the ghetto was much worse than I had imagined. On the good side, the house which we were ordered to go to was in a nice, leafy street, but away from the centre of town. It was large: not as large as my grandparents' but larger than ours. It had a garden with a couple of trees.

When we entered the house, however, there was much noise and confusion: people were rushing around, shouting names and arguing. Scuffles broke out for a better room. I was terrified and would not let go of my mother's hand. Dad explained that the three of us would be living in the same room; our kitchen and the bathroom would be shared with other families.

This was a nasty surprise. The only consolation was that I spotted Aunt Anna and Zsuzsi, since their room was in the same house. Later on that day, Grandma arrived and her luggage was carried by one of the men who had worked in the timber yard. "He refused the order not to help Jews," Grandma explained.

My mum tried to arrange things to create our new home. Dad unpacked the luggage, while I went to explore the rest of the house.

I did not like what I saw.

The kitchen was small and the bathroom already dirty. When I got back to our room I asked my dad, "How long are we going to stay here?"

"I don't know. As long as we are ordered."

"And where are we going from here?"

Dad looked at my mum who answered, "No one knows. We have to be patient. Why don't you find Zsuzsi and play with her? Later we'll all visit Grandma. Is that all right?"

It was not all right. I hated the ghetto, but I went to play with Zsuzsi. We thought of joining the other couple of children in the garden, but we changed our minds. We didn't like them: they were noisy and not very friendly.

Later in the evening we went to visit Grandma, who had a room on the first floor in another house. It was very small, but somehow she shrank to fit into it. She didn't look well, and for the first time I saw an old woman and not the forceful head of the family I had known.

When Dad asked how she was, however, her answer was curt: "I'm all right, thank you. Don't worry about me. You just look after your family."

When my mum and I were alone, I asked, "Why doesn't Grandma like Dad?"

She was surprised by my question and hesitated before answering. "She likes him, in her own way. But she had the idea that I should have married a rich man. And your dad wasn't rich. Now you know."

Well, not really, I thought, but I would ask again when I was older.

When Dad returned, Mum prepared cheese sandwiches and we went to the kitchen to eat, but there was already a family of six sitting round the table. I recognized the children from the garden. Defeated, we returned to our room, which felt small and sad compared to our own house, and had our first meal in the ghetto.

After breakfast every morning, my mother made regular visits to the market. To break the boredom of the days I asked her to take me with her, just so that I could get out of the ghetto.

Our little excursions became even more interesting when Aunt Anna and Zsuzsi joined us. We also tried to get some food for Grandma, who decided not to leave. "I have never been to the market to buy food for myself in my whole life and I am *not* starting now," she said.

In the previous year, I remembered, I had been fascinated by the variety of vegetables and fruits on the market stalls, which changed with the seasons: punnets of red strawberries and even redder raspberries in late spring; yellow apricots, blue and purple plums, pyramids of melons and watermelons, peaches with velvety skin and pale green pears in the summer; apples, fat quinces and squashy medlars in the autumn. It was such a pleasure to see all these things and an even greater pleasure to eat them. There had also been eggs, chicken, ducks and geese – and onions, the most famous produce of the town, apparently the best in Europe.

I had looked forward to these excursions, but now that we lived in the ghetto we had to start early. My mother explained: "Jews are allowed to go to the market to buy food only at a specified time. From nine thirty to eleven in the morning. If we arrive late, the best will have already gone, with not much left. And even then, there isn't much choice. We have to buy what we can get." She was right: everything

27

was so different now, with the stalls hardly displaying anything at all.

As the weather became warmer at the beginning of June, I asked Dad whether we could go to the river. Just outside town there was a beautiful river called the Maros. Going to the river had always been quite the adventure! The previous summer, Dad had started to teach me to swim. He had put me on the luggage rack of his bicycle, telling me firmly that I should hold on to him, with my arms round his waist so as not to fall off, while Gyuri followed us, cycling behind.

The river was quite near to our house: it didn't take more than fifteen or twenty minutes to get there.

Turning into the main road, we'd soon reached the last houses of town and continued on the dyke which protected the town from flooding in the spring. The most exciting part of the journey was cycling on this raised dyke with a view of the spires of the town on the left and the small forest, hiding the river, on the right.

After a short ride, Dad had got off and wheeled the bicycle down to the beginning of the path in the forest. I had remained sitting as still as I could, careful not to lose my balance, but Gyuri was braver and cycled down, ignoring Dad's protests.

When we arrived at the river, Dad had paid for us to use the wooden cabins that ran along the bank. We changed into our swimming trunks and, after lying on big towels to cool down, we waded into the water. There were two wooden barriers composed of round logs chained together in the river: the first marked the edge of the area for learners, while the second in deeper water showed how far good swimmers could go.

It was at the first barrier that Dad had started to teach me what he said was breaststroke. He put his hand under my tummy when he saw that I was going to sink. I had a glance at Gyuri swimming fast at the second barrier and saw that he was doing something different.

"It's front crawl," Dad explained. "He's a good swimmer, but I still don't like it when he swims out of my sight. You must always remember that this river is dangerous and has a very fast current."

By the end of my first lesson, I was very tired, but I had gradually got better. After the swim, we went ashore to dry off in the sun. Dad produced some sandwiches Mum had made and, later in the season, we had delicious corn on the cob, still warm when we ate it.

It was at the river that Dad explained how my grandparents had started their business. We saw a boat carrying large logs of wood and Dad pointed at it: "Do you see that boat? It's probably carrying logs to our timber yard. They cut the trees upstream, and the river is ideal for transport."

"What happens next?"

"They unload on to a truck which carries the logs to the timber yard."

"Did this make Grandma and Grandad rich?"

"Well, your grandad was very clever, and he bought modern equipment from Germany. You saw the engine room?" I nodded. "With this he beat his competitors to become the largest firm of this type in the county."

They had been happy times, but this year, in the ghetto, was different. When I asked my dad whether we could go to the river, he flatly refused.

"The changing rooms aren't open yet," he told me.

"To Jews," I heard my mother add in a whisper.

Staying in the ghetto was really boring. Everything was crowded and the tiny garden became too dirty to play in. After breakfast, I went to the market with my mum, but for the rest of the day there was very little I could do, so I often went to see Grandma with her.

After one visit, Mum told Dad that Grandma looked poorly, and she was worried about her health.

"Why don't you take her to see a doctor?" Dad asked.

"You must know her by now; she won't even hear of it," my mother replied.

After midday, Mum prepared lunch when the kitchen was not occupied by other families. In the afternoon we met Aunt Anna and Zsuzsi. She, like me, hated the ghetto. We wanted to play, but there was very little we could do. We missed our toys and the garden where we could run about and the vast space of the timber yard.

One day in June the monotony of our days was broken by some excitement. Rumours were spreading like wildfire throughout the ghetto, lifting the general gloom, that the Allies had landed in France.

I did not understand what this meant and had to ask my parents. Dad answered, "The Allies are the countries fighting the Germans: America, Great Britain and the Soviet Union. The fact that the Americans and British have landed in France means that Germany is now attacked not only by the Soviets from the East but also by the Allies from the West."

"Does it mean that the Germans are going to lose the war?" I asked. I had begun to dislike the Germans and was all for their defeat. I learned from my parents' conversations that they were the cause of all our troubles.

31

"Well, we don't know, but we hope, yes, that they are going to lose. It also means that we might go home sooner."

This cheered me up. I wanted to go home. Back to our house, back to my toys and back to playing with Zsuzsi. Of course, I did not know, nor did my father, how wrong he was. Going to the ghetto was only the beginning of what would turn out to be a long journey. Mum told me that we hadn't been in the ghetto for even a month, but it seemed much longer.

Chapter 3

Leaving Hungary

In mid-June, my mother told me we had to pack, since we were going to travel to Szeged.

I knew that Szeged was a large town and even knew that it had a famous university – the same university Gyuri couldn't go to, because he was Jewish. *It will be a short journey*, I thought, *it's not very far: only thirty kilometres from Makó.* I had only been there once before, with my parents, when they went to do some shopping for things they could not get in Makó.

First, we were told that we couldn't take everything from the ghetto with us, only suitcases and parcels not exceeding fifty kilograms. I didn't know how much that was, but Dad said I would see when they had finished packing.

"We can take one suit or dress, one change of underwear and one pair of shoes," my mum explained.

"Not very generous," Dad commented. "Fortunately, we can pack some bed linen and blankets."

"Yes," Mum answered, and even as she said this, she was already putting these things into a suitcase. "We can also take food which doesn't go off: tea, coffee, rice, biscuits and alcohol. No jewellery, money or other valuables. And no writing materials."

It was then that Mum turned to Dad and said, "We don't have any money to hide, but I've got a couple of pieces of jewellery: a bracelet and a pair of earrings my mother gave me when we got married. And the necklace you bought me for our tenth wedding anniversary. I could ask our neighbour, Mrs Szabó, who's always been very friendly, to keep these for us…"

"Don't you think that it's risky for her? She might end up in trouble for helping Jews."

"I can ask her anyway. She's free to say no … but you're right." Then Mum turned to me. "You haven't heard what we were talking about, okay? If you tell other people…"

Once we had finished packing, we had to leave the ghetto. We were marched towards the station accompanied by several gendarmes. They looked frightening in their military uniforms and helmets decorated with shiny cockerel's feathers.

In front of our synagogue, we were stopped. The gendarmes ordered the women to enter the building without any luggage. My mum disappeared with the other women, including Aunt Anna and Grandma, while I waited outside with my dad and all the men and children.

After a short time, the women started to come out, but there was no sign of my mother. Finally, she came back to us. She looked upset: her dress was untidy and even her face had changed.

"What happened?" Dad asked. Mum whispered something in reply. She clearly didn't want me to hear it, and I caught some words but I didn't understand: "examination ... very humiliating..."

Then I heard a full sentence, since she was so angry she could not restrain her voice any more: "My own doctor supervised it, and that was the worst thing." It was only much later that I was to understand the full details of what had happened and why my mother was so upset.

Dad hugged her and we continued our march in the midst of the crowds of people. When we arrived at the station, another surprise was waiting for us. I thought that we were going to travel on a nice passenger train, but I couldn't see one anywhere. My hopes of sitting in a comfortable compartment with my parents and looking out of a large window at the ever-changing countryside disappeared. The train at the station was composed not of passenger carriages, but wagons usually used for transporting animals. The windows were small and each was barred by iron rods.

Surely this couldn't be the train we were going to be travelling on?

We remained on the platform, with all the other people, waiting for a proper train to arrive. We didn't know what to do. However, the gendarmes left us in no doubt. They began to shout orders in a very threatening way to get us into the wagons: "Dirty Jews, what are you waiting for? Get on, and quick!"

And to give the orders even greater emphasis, they started to use their truncheons on those who were too slow to climb up the steep steps of the wagons. We were forced by the gendarmes to embark.

It was the first but not the last time that I was frightened.

Mum climbed in first and Dad lifted me into her outstretched arms. Our wagon soon became so crowded that we could only stand: there was hardly any space to move, let alone to sit down on the floor.

I wanted to cry, but held back my tears.

Mum looked at me and said, "It won't be a long journey. It shouldn't take more than an hour." Still looking frightened, she added, "You'll see." Then she turned to my dad and said, "I can't believe that we're being forced to pay for this journey."

"Oh, yes," Dad answered, "the mayor is a real..."

And he used a word that I was shocked to hear.

"Don't use that word," Mum started to reply.

But he interrupted. "Do you have a better one?"

I didn't know what they were talking about, until Dad explained. "It's not enough that they forced us out of our homes, it's not enough that they stole everything we had, but they've even charged us for a journey we don't want to make."

"Calm down; there's no point in getting upset," was my mum's answer.

For ages the train did not move. It took a long time to force everybody into the crowded wagons. The sun was becoming hot, and standing close like sardines was very uncomfortable. People were shoving and pushing to secure their space, as the gendarmes forced more and more passengers into the already overcrowded wagon.

To make things worse for me, Mum had made me wear more clothes than was comfortable for summer, so that our luggage didn't exceed the allowed weight.

Finally, the train slowly pulled out of the station. In a

few minutes, as the engine gathered speed, we crossed the Maros. I said goodbye to the river and summer swims, which now seemed a long time ago.

My mother was wrong when she said that the journey would be short. It felt very long. It might have helped if we'd had a view, but there wasn't even a chance of a quick glimpse at the countryside. I was pressed between my parents, and the only things I could see were Mum's skirt and Dad's trousers.

The train stopped at last, and the door of the wagon was opened. Everybody became impatient to get off, and my mum had to protect me with her body so that I didn't get squashed. It was a long time before everyone was on the ground.

At the station there was another group of gendarmes waiting for us who were no friendlier than those we had left behind in Makó. They ordered us to get into lines. We obeyed but didn't know what would happen next. From the station, we had to march to a football stadium, which fortunately was not very far.

As we arrived, I was amazed to see hundreds of tents on the grass. I didn't know why they were there, but it soon became clear. One of the tents was allocated to us by the ever-present gendarmes. Those who had arrived earlier were put up in the changing rooms and storage spaces, while some people occupied the terraces.

Since I had never slept in a tent before, I was quite excited. Our tent was completely empty, with no bedding or anything. Dad looked into a couple of neighbouring ones and reported that they had nothing inside either. *Sleeping in a tent in summer is going to be fun*, I thought, as we occupied our new home.

However, it turned out differently. A storm broke during the night. First, there was only distant thunder, but as this became louder and louder it became more and more frightening. Then the downpour started, accompanied by bursts of lightning. Soon our tent was flooded. My parents tried to keep our suitcases dry.

During that first night away, we hardly slept. In the morning I was exhausted. After the night's storm, the sun rose the next morning, and I surveyed the football ground with Dad. It was boring to wait around all day for nothing to happen. Worse, we had lost track of Aunt Anna and Zsuzsi and there was no one at all I could play with. After a couple of nights, we were told we were going to be transferred to a deserted brick factory. I was happy to leave, as there wasn't much to do. Time passed very slowly with nothing to look at and nowhere to go.

On the way to the factory, we crossed a bridge over a river which was much wider than the Maros. When I asked Dad which river it was, he replied, "It's the Tisza. The Maros flows into this river and in turn the Tisza flows into the Danube, the longest river in Europe."

"How long is the Danube?"

"I knew you would ask," my father replied. "I don't know precisely, but a couple of thousand kilometres long. Don't even think of swimming the length of it."

On arrival at the brick factory, we were happy to find Grandma, Aunt Anna and Zsuzsi again. The last time we had seen them had been at the railway station in Makó. For the next couple of days more and more people arrived in the factory, until it became crowded. Here, at least we could sleep in a large empty shed. My mother tried to separate us from other families, without much success. She marked out our sleeping places on the floor with our luggage.

"Why are there so many people here?"

Dad explained that Szeged had become a collection centre for Jews from all the surrounding areas. When I asked how long we were going to stay, he answered that he didn't know. I was disappointed that my parents didn't seem to know much more about our journey than I did.

Zsuzsi and I set out on a discovery tour of the factory. It

was a large space with sheds and an enormous chimney, but the only sign of what this factory had once produced were small collections of bricks.

The nastiest part of the tour was the discovery of the latrine. It was the first time we had seen such a thing, and if we had any doubt about its function, the surrounding stench betrayed it from quite far away. In the summer heat it was horrid. During our stay, I tried to pee anywhere where I thought I would not be seen – just to escape the latrine. But for other things, it was impossible to avoid it and every morning my mum came with me.

As Zsuzsi and I were walking around, two gendarmes suddenly appeared. "What are you doing here without your parents?" one of them asked in a way that nearly made my heart stop. We were so frightened we just stood without answering.

"Can't you speak?" one of them asked. We waited to be beaten but instead we were told to get back to our parents as soon as we could. We ran away as fast as possible. Mum was very angry. We were told that we should not wander around and disappear from their sight.

While we were staying at the factory, my mum found it difficult to keep us clean. Although we still had a bar of soap, there was a water shortage, so she rubbed me down with a wet towel. By the time she had finished, the towel had dried in the heat. I also started to miss my favourite shirts and jumpers and shorts. When I asked Mum when I could wear them again, she said she would buy even nicer ones when we got home. Hearing this I nearly cried, since no one seemed to know *when* we would get home.

We must have been in the brick factory for about ten days, and I was getting increasingly bored. However, at the end of June, we were asked to go to the large, open space in the centre of the factory. An official, holding something to his mouth which looked like the large funnel Mum used occasionally in the kitchen, announced that everybody was going to leave.

I asked Mum what the man was holding. She said that it was a megaphone, a simple instrument which increases the volume of sound.

"*Mega* means large and *phone* means sound," Dad added, "so the word *megaphone*—"

But before he could finish, I blurted out: "Big sound."

"Bright lad," he said.

After the announcement, no one seemed to know where we were going. Then everything happened so fast that I couldn't follow what was going on. I heard my parents arguing about some lists – but what they were for, I had no idea.

When I asked, my dad tried to explain. "The commandant in charge of the brick factory has asked the leaders of Jewish communities, including those of our town, to give a complete list of all the people from where they live."

"What for?"

"To organize our transport."

"So we're leaving?"

"Yes, maybe as soon as tomorrow."

"With Grandma, Aunt Anna and Zsuzsi?" I asked. Suddenly I was worried that I might lose Zsuzsi's company.

"Yes, I hope so. We must stay together as a family," my mum replied. "They originally demanded that those under twelve and over fifty should have a separate list and travel on a different train."

"Ili, please don't make it more complicated than it needs to be for the boy."

I immediately knew that something unusual was going on, since my dad hardly ever used the short form of Mum's name: she was always Ilona to him.

"It's the most important thing that the family is not broken up," my mum said.

"Yes, I agree," said Dad.

I interrupted to ask, "Where are we going?"

"We don't know," my mum answered, "but there are rumours that we might be leaving Hungary."

I didn't know what was outside Hungary but was excited by the idea of travelling so far. "Which country?" I asked.

"It's not certain, but probably Germany or Poland," said my dad.

In the end, it was neither. And at that point, I didn't know just how lucky we were that our destination turned out to be different.

My parents learned that everybody in the ghetto was on an official list and that there would be three trains. Everybody would be told which train they were travelling on. Dad went to find out. When he came back, he said that we were allocated to train number two with Grandma.

"And Anna and Zsuzsi?" Mum asked.

"I didn't ask, but even if I had, they wouldn't have told me."

We soon found out. Aunt Anna came to tell us that they were on train number one. When Mum told her that we were not on their train, she asked my parents to try to get on to the same one, that we should all travel together.

After she had left, my parents argued, but in the end decided that we should stay on train number two. I protested that I wanted to travel on Zsuzsi's train, but my parents would not change their minds. Later they told Aunt Anna of their decision. Trying to change our train would create complications and we should avoid drawing attention to ourselves at the last minute.

So we stayed on our train.

In the meantime, Aunt Anna asked the officials whether they could join us on our train, but she was flatly refused.

Their train left first.

That was the last time we saw Aunt Anna or Zsuzsi.

It was a very hot day. We were marched to the station, which was not very far. Then we were forced and pushed into the wagons. When I asked my parents again where we were going, they repeated that they didn't know. The wagon was full, but more and more people were forced inside. Then the door was shut and there was a loud bang as the wagon was locked. Suddenly it became much darker, with the only light coming through a couple of small, barred windows. We stood there for a long time, but the train remained stationary.

I heard Dad telling my mum that there were more than eighty passengers in our wagon: mostly adults and old people but also children like me. Everyone was standing quite close together and bumping into each other, as the train finally moved out of the station. It was very uncomfortable. Suddenly I wanted to pee, but there was nowhere to go. Asking people around us, my mum pushed her way through, dragging me by my hand. In one corner of the wagon there were two large buckets. One contained water, the other already had some foul-smelling yellowish-brown liquid in it.

"Do I have to pee into this?" I asked.

"Yes, there's no choice," Mum told me.

As it became darker, Mum gave us some bread and cheese, but I was still hungry. I asked for more, but she refused: "I don't know how long the journey will last; we must keep some for tomorrow."

The wagon gradually became completely dark: it must have been night. Occasional lights by the railway tracks flashed by. There was not much air, and a woman standing next to us, who was even older than my mum, fell. The wagon was so crowded that she didn't hit the floor, but as people tried to make space, she gradually slid down. No one seemed to take any notice though.

It felt like the journey would never end.

I don't know how long we travelled for, but it must have

been, or seemed to be, a couple of days. This was not the exciting journey abroad I had expected. It was terribly boring, since I couldn't do anything at all.

I couldn't even move.

We had to stand the whole time, but I was close to my mother, so I tried to sleep – until the movement of the train woke me up with a jolt. After a while I did not know whether I was awake or in a nightmare: it all became blurred.

Finally, the train came to an unexpected halt. We thought it was just one of those stops on the open tracks (of which there had been many), but we must have arrived, since the wagon door was opened.

What a relief! We could finally breathe some fresh air.

We were eager to leave the wagon, but as it emptied, a couple of passengers remained lying on the floor, including the woman who had fallen next to us.

Soldiers in uniform were waiting for us and shouted in a language I didn't understand. They also wore uniforms I had not seen before: different from the gendarmes'.

"*Raus! Raus! Schnell, schnell!*"

"We must have arrived in Germany," Mum said. "It means: 'Out, out, faster, faster.'" I found out during the following months that my mother spoke fluent German.

This was how I learned that we had left Hungary. I felt excited. *At school, whenever I get there,* I thought, *I'll be able to tell the other children that I have been abroad.*

Soon after our arrival, we spotted Grandma in the crowd. She had travelled in a different wagon. I noticed that she had changed. She could hardly walk and breathed with difficulty.

I looked at a big sign in strange lettering. Although I recognized most letters, since my mum had started to teach me before school, this sign defeated me.

"What does it say? I can't read it."

"It says: STRASSHOF. Do you see the other, smaller sign, in the shape of an arrow? It has 'Wiener Neustadt' on it. This is the first good news for a long time," Dad added.

"Why?" I asked.

"Because we aren't in Germany, but in Austria. The name means Viennese Newtown. Vienna or Wien, the capital, must be near."

"Why is that good?"

"Well, Austria, although it's now part of Germany, is a different country and it's nearer to Hungary. Many years ago, Hungary and Austria were both part of a big empire."

"What happened?"

"Look," Dad said, "we don't have time for a history

lesson, you'll learn all about it at school."

He was right, since he had hardly finished the sentence before two soldiers rushed towards us, shouting and pointing with their truncheons at people who were already lined up in front of a low building.

Chapter 4

In the Vienna Woods

We were ordered to line up to register. The soldiers had lists of our names and, as we said who we were, they ticked us off.

And then we waited and waited.

I started on a little discovery tour, but my mother called me back immediately. After a while we were told that there was no space for us inside the makeshift buildings and that we would have to sleep outside on the grass.

It was a warm summer evening; the sun had just disappeared behind the trees. I looked forward to this new adventure: I had never slept under the sky. In Szeged we had slept in a tent and now we were going to sleep in the open air. It was going to be fun! We were given something to eat, and we went to lie down. For the first time, I could watch the stars in the ink-blue sky until I fell asleep.

In the morning, Mum woke me up and I immediately

noticed she had been crying. Without me having to ask, she told me: "Your Grandma died during the night." She started sobbing.

I must have looked as if I hadn't heard, because Dad added, "Her heart just stopped, according to a doctor."

I knew that Grandma was old, but I just could not imagine she would die.

"What are we doing now?" I asked.

"We've been told there can be no funeral, but we can pray for her. Come to see her for the last time."

"Do I have to?"

"Yes," said Mum.

I followed my parents and saw Grandma lying peacefully on her back on a blanket in the grass. Later, men came to join us and dug a grave. They prayed, and that was it.

I did not think of Grandma, but of Zsuzsi. I knew that with her I could have discussed Grandma's death more openly than with my parents. Despite being frightened of Grandma, just like me, Zsuzsi also loved her.

The next day, we were ordered to line up again and people in civilian clothes came to look at us slowly and carefully. They even returned for a second time. This reminded me of my mother looking at some goods she wanted to buy at the market.

"They are local Austrians from Wiener Neustadt, the town down the road, and they are looking for able people to work for them," my mum explained.

After a while two men, one old and one young, stopped in front of us and pointed at us. The elder said something to my parents, which I could not understand. With Mum holding my hand, we stepped out of line to follow them.

"We are going to work for them," Mum said.

"What are we going to do?"

"We don't know yet, but soon we're going to find out," Dad said.

Following in their footsteps, we carried our luggage until we reached an open lorry on the road. The two men told my parents to get on the back. I was pulled up by my dad, while Mum lifted me from the road.

This was getting even more exciting: I had never travelled on a lorry. We sat on a makeshift wooden bench along the side of the lorry. The road was bumpy, but the ride was fun. We drove through a forest and arrived in Wiener Neustadt.

The lorry pulled up in a street; we got off and carried our luggage inside. As I looked around, I nearly cried out since the place reminded me so much of our timber yard at home. In the large courtyard there were machines, but instead of piles of timber, there were large columns of bricks. In one corner there was a building which looked like our office and a couple of small houses. It was into one of these that the two men directed us.

As my parents opened our luggage, my mum explained that this was the place where we were going to live and that the two men, father and son, were owners of a small building firm. More importantly, she said, here we would have our own room.

There was a large washroom for everybody in the barracks. It was empty, and we rushed in to clean ourselves from the filth of the journey. The water was ice cold, and I dreamed of my hot bath at home, but after I had been scrubbed clean by my mum I felt clean and so much better.

For dinner, we had a hot stew with a lot more potato than meat. However, it was the best meal we'd eaten since we'd left home. And it was so comfortable to lie in a proper bed, even if the mattress was very hard.

Next morning, after a breakfast of coffee with a slice of bread and jam, my mum told me that we were going to work. When I asked what sort of work, she said, "I don't know precisely, but we're going to repair roads. This town has been a target for the Allies," she continued, "because there is a large factory which produces aeroplanes for the Germans.

The roads are also bombed to stop transport to and from the factory. The damage needs repair."

"Am I going to work too?" I asked.

"You'll come with us, but of course you aren't going to work."

"What am I going to do all day?"

"I don't know, but there will be other children and you can play with them. Wait and see."

After breakfast, we were picked up by the same lorry which had transported us from Strasshof. Several other people, including a couple of children, joined us. They were also from Hungary and had travelled on the same train as us.

"You see," Mum said as we made our way on to the lorry, "I told you that there would be other children for you to play with."

The lorry drove us through town, and we soon reached open fields. Turning back, we could see the spire of the church.

After a short while, the lorry stopped and we all got off. My parents, along with the rest of the adult passengers, were given tools. I didn't recognize them all, but they included large spades – so large that I couldn't lift them. The owner's son, who was driving the lorry, pointed to a small stretch of damaged road with a big hole in the middle. This was what had to be repaired.

One of the boys who was a little bit taller than me, with shiny brown hair and large brown eyes, looked me up and down, and after a minute or two of hesitation introduced himself.

"My name is Gábor," he said, "but you can call me Gabi." This was the beginning of our friendship.

Unfortunately, what we could do was limited, although the fields on either side of the road our parents were repairing gave us the chance to explore. We played hide-and-seek in the nearby copse, but I was discouraged from disappearing into the trees by my mother, who wanted to keep me within her sight. We arranged running competitions, which I didn't win but enjoyed competing in. We also played hopscotch. At my request, Dad drew the squares on to a preserved stretch of the road.

Soon, our days had a regular order: early wake-up, often in the dark; quick wash in the bathroom; breakfast of coffee and a slice of bread with jam or cheese or sausage; on to the lorry; work for the adults while we tried to invent games and played; short break for lunch and a quick bite for those who saved some food from breakfast; work until sunset; drive back; dinner and early bed.

After a couple of months this had become boring, but

the good thing was that not much danger threatened us. The only threat came from the sky. The air raids, the enemy planes coming to bomb us, became more and more frequent, but they also became part of our lives.

It was summer and the fields beside the road were full of wildflowers. We collected these and tried to make colourful bouquets, which we gave to our mothers.

However, chasing butterflies was the most fun. The wildflowers attracted butterflies and bees. The latter we avoided. The butterflies, landing on a flower or a leaf, seemed to be an easy catch. How wrong we were! Whenever we thought we had got them, they always escaped at the last moment. The only time I caught one, I regretted it, since its beauty became powder in my fist.

At dusk, the lorry would return to drive us back to the camp. After washing ourselves as well as possible, we had dinner. There was a severe shortage of food, and we got less and less as the days and months passed by.

Occasionally we received some additional food from unexpected sources. One morning, as the lorry drove us to another stretch of the road, we saw a farm in the distance. My mum discovered that this farm had a pigsty, and the farmer filled the troughs with swill which also contained some damaged potatoes. On one occasion, when we had arrived before the pigs were let out, Mum fished out the best ones for us to eat and cooked them later. The farmer must have spotted this, since next time we found a couple of large, cooked potatoes on a piece of newspaper.

Occasionally, when I was walking in the street, a door would open and I would be gently pulled in by an unknown woman. She would look around to make sure that nobody could see us. Then she would give me a slice of bread and a glass of milk. By that time, I knew how to say thank you in German: "*Danke schön.*"

Unexpectedly we also made friends with a local man. Franz was about my dad's age, and he arrived one evening on an old bike.

Franz talked to my parents, and they seemed to be cheered up by his appearance. After he had left, my mum explained: "His son died in the war: frozen to death in Russia. Franz was a teacher, but he lost his job because he protested against the war. He told us that the Germans are losing and it won't last long now. Paris was liberated by the Americans a week ago."

"Where's Paris?"

"It's the capital of France."

"So the Americans are going to liberate us too?"

"I wish they would," Dad interrupted, "but Paris is a very long way from here."

The next time our new friend arrived, he wanted to see me. He gave me a set of beautiful crayons and a notebook.

"It's for you to draw in," my mum translated. He also told Mum that the set had been his son's.

I was very happy with my new notebook and crayons and often drew in the evenings. I drew the house in which we lived, the field with the flowers and butterflies and the planes bombing the town. I tried to draw my parents repairing the road, but the picture wasn't very good.

Unfortunately, the man's visits soon stopped. He told Mum that the owners of the factory had ordered him to stay away, that he shouldn't visit us again. I was very sorry. Although I couldn't talk with him myself, I missed his visits.

In the autumn, the air raids became more frequent. One day, when the sirens started to sound their prolonged, ear-splitting warnings, the lorry arrived to collect us. We ran as fast as we could and climbed up into it. As soon as the last worker got on, the driver sped away and drove us to an air-raid shelter in the garden of the building firm. It was dark and musty, and it might once have been a wine cellar. Empty wine bottles sat on the shelves and there were corks all over the floor.

On another occasion, my mum and I missed the lorry.

When the sirens began to sound, we ran as fast as we could, but by the time we got to the pick-up point, the lorry had disappeared. We didn't know what to do. Not far from the road there were a couple of trees, and we ran to find shelter underneath. I lay on my tummy and my mum put one of her arms around me and partly covered my body with hers: as if to protect me from the bombs.

We heard the distant hum of planes, which intensified into an ear-splitting roar as they passed overhead.

We expected the worst. But nothing happened.

The planes disappeared as unexpectedly as they had arrived, without dropping a single bomb on the road. We heard distant explosions: they must have dropped the bombs over the town.

Then we heard the roar of a single plane.

Suddenly Mum said, "Turn over. If we have to die, at least we'll be able to see the bombs."

I turned over and looked up, waiting for the bombs to strike. But no bombs fell. Instead, shimmering strips of light descended from the blue sky, billowing in the breeze. We didn't know what they were. We left the trees and slowly walked into the open field.

The shimmering lights were millions and millions

of thin strips of aluminium foil, which kept coming and coming. I collected a large handful and made a ball.

Mum didn't know what they were or why they were falling from the sky either. Only later in the evening did the owner of the business tell us that they were meant to interfere with radio communication. But for me it remained magic, and my shiny ball became the envy of all the other children.

As summer turned into autumn, the weather got colder and the days became shorter. One day, the owners of the building firm told us that our work had ended. We were asked to pack. The same day they drove us back to Strasshof, to the same place where we had arrived from Hungary.

However, Strasshof was now completely different. Not only had the weather turned cold, with the summer heat long gone, but the noisy, milling crowds had also disappeared. There weren't many people around at all.

Soon after our arrival, we were directed to the barracks. Just as well, since it froze and snowed during the night. By morning the world had turned white. My parents told me that it was the end of November.

We did not stay in Strasshof for long. After a couple of days, we were ordered to march to the station and forced, yet again, into wagons. When I asked my parents where we were going, they said they didn't know.

By now I should have learned that, although they might be far cleverer than I was, they didn't know any more about our destinations than I did. It was the beginning of yet another journey into the unknown.

Chapter 5

Arriving in Bergen-Belsen

The journey from Strasshof was unlike any of our previous journeys. The weather made all the difference. Instead of the burning heat of summer, when we nearly suffocated in the airless wagons, now we would have frozen to death if the warmth of so many people hadn't saved us. I also benefitted from the warm overcoat my mother had packed for me back at home.

The wagon was very crowded. Again, Dad told me that there must have been at least seventy people, maybe more. He was an accountant, so he must have been right. We ran out of the little food we had brought, and I was increasingly hungry. More hungry than ever before.

I was also terribly bored and got very tired of standing. I tried to stand on one leg at a time, changing from left to right and from right to left. Then Mum suggested that I should try to sit down between her and Dad's legs, practically on their shoes. That was much better.

After a never-ending journey, the train came to a final stop. I didn't know how long we had been travelling – it felt like we would *never* arrive. But, finally, we did.

There was silence. Then we heard shouting in German and dogs barking. The door of our wagon was opened and a bitterly cold wind blew in. However unpleasant, it was much better than the stench inside: the buckets we'd been using as toilets had been overflowing.

"*Raus, raus! Schneller, schneller!*" By this point, I had heard these words so many times that I understood what they meant: "Out, out! Faster, faster!"

First Dad climbed out, then Mum lifted me and handed me to Dad. Finally, she joined us.

As before, not everybody left, as after the wagon was emptied several bodies were found on the floor.

Mum turned my head away.

"We're in Bergen," she said, looking at the station's sign. The letters were written in the same strange way as those at the station in Strasshof. In Austria, when I saw shop names in this kind of lettering, Mum told me that these were Gothic characters. I had never seen letters like these in Hungary.

"Wherever Bergen is," my dad added.

"Soon, we're going to find out," Mum answered.

And we did. We were lined up and ordered to march. It was freezing cold, and after the artificial warmth of the wagon, the wind was razor sharp.

I kept asking my parents how long we had to walk for, but they didn't know. Mum tried to keep me warm, pulling me closer to her body.

We passed houses and gardens under snow. The German soldiers kept shouting, "Faster, faster!" and those who slowed down were pushed forward or beaten. After a long and exhausting march, we finally arrived.

Dad looked around slowly, as if taking in all the sights. Finishing his survey, he remained silent. We both looked at him, waiting and prompting an answer to explain what we were doing here in the middle of nowhere, in the freezing winter.

Then he said something that I could barely hear: "This is a concentration camp."

My mother remained silent.

"What is a concentration camp?" I asked.

"It's a place where Jews are forced to live," my father responded.

"So it's a prison," I said.

"Yes, it's a sort of prison," my mum agreed.

Looking around, I saw a collection of low buildings which vaguely reminded me of the houses in Strasshof, but this place was much more frightening.

The whole camp was surrounded by metal fences with lots of barbed wire on top. At regular intervals there were tall watchtowers with soldiers in them. I could see their machine guns in the one nearest to us.

The camp looked enormous. I had never seen such a large place before. There were many houses, but somehow, they were not real houses. Not houses like those back home and not even like I had seen in Wiener Neustadt. They were all the same, very low, and must have been built in a hurry. There were paths, partly covered by melting snow, but I could see no paved roads inside the camp.

In the distance I spotted trees, and the sight cheered me up. I thought I'd be able to explore the grounds after we had settled in, but I was to be thoroughly disappointed.

After a moment or two Mum said, "KZ Lager Bergen-Belsen." Expecting my question, she added, "It means Bergen-Belsen Concentration Camp."

Now I knew its name as well. "But why has it got two names?"

My mother explained: "Bergen was the town where we

arrived, as you saw, and Belsen was the small village we walked through to get here."

There was disorder and shouting, with people rushing around. Some were desperately searching for relatives they had lost during the journey. No one knew at first what to do and where to go. Everybody was carrying their luggage, including my parents. These were the only remaining pieces of our previous life.

Then a couple of men appeared, who ordered us to line up in Hungarian. They must have arrived before us, since they seemed to know everything. One shouted, "Once you are registered you will be allocated to the different barracks. But before that you all have to go through disinfection."

"What's disinfection?" I asked.

"I knew you'd ask," said my dad. "It's a process which makes sure that we don't carry infectious agents, like bugs which cause disease."

"What are they going to do to us?"

"We don't know, but you'll see."

And we did. Near to the entrance of the camp was a building, larger and more solid that the barracks. We were ordered to enter, with the men separated from the women and children, and someone shouted in Hungarian, "Get undressed! Take everything off! Your clothes will be treated by hot air to kill the lice." It was the first time I had heard this word, but later we had many closer encounters with these "lice". At the end we had an unexpected treat: a warm shower in the same building.

"At least we have a sort of bathroom," my mother said. However, this was the first and last time we got anywhere near to a proper bathroom with hot water.

The odd buildings all around were called barracks. They were quite low, long and neatly regimented – different from all the houses I had seen before. I did not like them. And I liked them even less when I finally saw inside.

Suddenly soldiers appeared, and, using their truncheons, they managed to line us up within a couple minutes. They were wearing black uniforms with the letters "SS" on the collars, and to make it even more frightening: a skull with two crossbones.

Mum and I managed to make our way close to my dad again. I asked him who these men were, and he explained: "They're special soldiers, the so-called SS guard. The two letters stand for two German words, which mean 'protection unit'. They were originally Hitler's bodyguards, but now they number a million and are the most savage force of the German Army." I was impressed by just how much my dad knew.

Our names, birthdates, places of birth and our home

addresses were all recorded by a man who was probably my father's age, but with a lot more hair. When my mum was about to speak for me, I interrupted her and, in a clear voice, told him my full name. "I was born on 22 October 1939 in Makó," I continued. "I am Hungarian. We live in Makó."

"You've got a clever son," said the man in Hungarian, who was writing in a large, lined book. My dad asked where we were, and the man quickly whispered, not to be noticed by anybody, that the concentration camp was in northern Germany. The next town was Celle and the nearest large city was Hanover. Dad asked what the date was. Having been travelling for days, we didn't know. "It's 7 December," said the man.

Hearing this, Mum said, "I can't believe we only left home six months ago."

"I know," Dad added, "it seems so much longer."

The man gave each of us a number.

Mum told me that I was Number 8431. She was 8517 and Dad 8432.

I didn't understand why we were numbered, but at this stage, I wasn't frightened, rather more curious about what was going to happen next.

We were told that we were going to stay in the so-called

Hungarians' Camp. They had started to arrive in large numbers in the summer. We must have been late arrivals.

When we entered the camp, we had seen some people, both men and women, wearing a strange uniform. I had never seen anything like it before. The uniforms were made of rough material with dark stripes. I didn't like the look of them at all.

When Mum enquired, she was told that we were not going to wear those ugly uniforms but could keep our own clothes on. Although we only had a few pieces of clothing and, by then, everything we had was worn out, I was happy not to be forced into the striped uniform many people in the camp had to wear.

We were all lined up again with the men separated from the women and children once more. I saw my dad disappearing with the other men. I asked my mother why we were being separated from him and she explained that the men would stay in the same camp but would live in different barracks.

Suddenly I was terrified that I was going to be separated from Mum too. At my anxious questioning she confirmed that I would stay with her.

We were then told to line up yet again, and a female guard came to survey us. She was tall and young, and was carrying a truncheon. She was not the first female guard I had seen, but she looked more frightening than those in Austria.

What happened next was the most horrible event of the whole journey. If I was ever under any illusion that we were on an adventure, by now that had completely disappeared. This was the first time I understood that our journey was not just an unusual adventure, but an unforeseen set of terrible events: each new surprise more frightening than the last. Our lives were in danger.

My mum was holding a small canvas bag, which she should have surrendered with our other luggage. The female SS guard who was watching us spotted the bag and ordered my mother to give it to her. Mum looked at her and said in a clear voice in German, "*Nein.*"

"It's my jewels," she said in Hungarian and then repeated it in German. I didn't understand why she was saying this, since all the jewellery and money we had owned had been taken away by the Hungarian gendarmes at the beginning of the journey.

Mum doesn't know what she's saying, I wanted to shout, but before I could, I saw the guard hitting her so hard that she fell backwards. As she fell, she dropped the bag. When it hit the ground, a single onion and a couple of shrivelled apples rolled out: the treasury of food she had been keeping for me.

Obeying the wave of the guard's truncheon, two women left the line and lifted my mum up. On the order of another guard, she was led away. I followed them, not knowing where we were going. I was determined not to let her out of my sight.

I started to talk to her: "Mum…" but she didn't answer and looked over my head. I realized with sudden horror that she didn't recognize me.

After a short walk, we ended up in a makeshift first aid room which, I learned later, was called the "hospital". A nurse came and examined my mother. She was also Hungarian and said, "Don't be frightened. I'm going to give an injection to your mother and she'll be all right. Many people have this sort of reaction on arrival after the long journey."

I thought she just wanted to calm me down, but she was right. After a short time, Mum came around. She didn't remember what had happened and I didn't dare remind her. The most important thing was that she recognized me and smiled at me, as if nothing had happened. Soon we left the hospital.

This is how our life in Belsen started.

*

Mum and I did what we had been told earlier and went to one of the barracks for women within the area of buildings kept for Hungarians. My mother told me it was barracks Number 11.

As we entered, I saw rows and rows of three-tiered bunk beds. Since we had arrived late, we had to climb up to an empty space on the top tier. I needed Mum's help to get up, but later, with frequent practice, I could manage on my own and even enjoyed this challenge.

The bed that I shared with my mother was not a real bed. It was a space covered by a hard mattress filled with straw and a thin blanket, not warm enough to protect us against the cold. Mum carefully separated our share of space, using the few belongings we still had to mark the border with the next "bed". Once Mum had given my dad his clothing, our little pile of possessions had shrunk even further. We climbed down and went out to discover the grounds outside.

First, we found the latrine, which we both had to use. I hated it at first sight. Since it was cold, clouds of steam rose from the ditch, carrying the stench far away.

During the coming months I grew to hate that latrine more than anything else in the camp – even more than the "bathroom", which turned out to be a large, partly opened shed and practically empty on our first visit. It was very different from the bathroom at home. On one wall ran a long water duct with several taps at regular intervals. I turned on one of the taps to try the temperature of the water but immediately withdrew my hands: the surprise was quite painful, since instead of the expected warmth, the water was ice cold. Yet during the next few months, I always had to wash myself in freezing water without complaining, under my mum's watchful eye.

Then we saw a building which had a chimney that was much, much taller than ordinary houses have. It reminded me of the chimney of the brick factory back in Szeged, but even that was shorter. We saw that dead bodies were being carried to the building. I couldn't help looking. The bodies didn't look very heavy. They looked a bit like sacks being lifted from one place to another.

"What's that building?" I asked, as I tried not to be scared.

"I'm not sure, but it's probably a crematorium."

"What's a crematorium?"

"Do you have to know everything?"

"Yes," I said without hesitation.

"It's a place where they burn dead bodies."

"Why don't they bury them?"

Mum hesitated before she answered, "The ground is too frozen to dig graves."

This was the first time I had seen so *many* dead people.

Of course, I remembered Grandma and the couple of bodies on the floor of the wagons at the end of each train journey. They were individual people who had died. But here it was very different. There were just too many. Apart from the ones being carried into the crematorium, there were more piled up on a cart: there must have been a dozen or more. Why had they died? I was too scared to ask.

On the first day in Belsen, I could not have known that much, much worse was coming.

So far, the first discoveries were very depressing. Everything was so much worse than in Austria.

"I hate it," I told my mother. I could see, or rather feel, that she was also unhappy.

"I know," she said, "but we can't do anything about it. We have to learn to endure."

"But how?"

"How to endure? By surviving day by day."

"And how long are we going to stay?"

"I don't know how long we're going to say, but with God's help, I hope not very long."

This was the first time I heard her calling on God. Since we were not very religious, I was surprised that Mum turned to God for help. I knew it meant we must be in danger.

By the time we returned to the barracks, it was pitch dark. However unpleasant the smell inside, it was at least warm. We got a piece of bread and cheese, which we carried to our bunk bed to eat there. It was not much, but I was terribly hungry, and it tasted good.

My mother tried to make our "bed" comfortable, but the space was limited. A few inches from our feet was someone else's "bed". The mattress was hard, and as night came, the barracks became even colder. I snuggled up to Mum for extra warmth. Soon I fell asleep and our first day in Bergen-Belsen Concentration Camp came to an end.

Chapter 6

Surviving in a concentration camp

In the morning, after we had climbed down from our bunk, we had our breakfast in the barracks. Breakfast most days consisted of a slice of bread and coffee: a brown liquid which tasted bitter and unpleasant. However, being hot, at least it warmed us up. Once we got the food, we stayed in the barracks, however crowded it was. Like most people, we climbed back on to our bunks or drank the coffee and ate the bread standing around. There were no benches to sit on, or tables to eat at, only the odd chair.

A couple of women who were also prisoners were in charge of distributing food, and Mum talked to them, hoping I might get a thicker slice of bread.

When there was time before, but in most cases after, breakfast, we paid our daily visit to the latrine and then to the "bathroom". It was always very early in the morning, and it was pitch dark and freezing cold. I could not get out fast enough, but Mum was very strict about cleaning me up as much as possible. After we'd been in the camp a few weeks, Mum added another odd procedure to our morning routine. I had to remove most of my clothing, which Mum carefully examined. When I was dressed again, she combed my hair and looked at my head very carefully as if she were counting each hair.

The first time she made me go through this, I asked her why she was doing it. Her reply was just one word, a word I had first heard when we arrived: "Lice."

"Lice?" I had only a vague idea that lice were something I should not have, but after her explanation I was left in no doubt.

"They carry disease, and we have to do everything we can not to get them. If you itch, tell me straight away."

"This is why we had to be dis…" I could not finish the word.

"Yes, this is why they *disinfected* us on arrival."

Despite all the precautions, we *had* picked up lice, and Mum remorselessly killed them by squeezing them to death between her nails. In the end, her war was successful: we got rid of them.

After breakfast, we were ordered to leave the barracks and line up outside. It was one of the senior prisoners, the barracks elder, who ordered us out; apparently, he was in charge of our barracks. Outside, we formed rows behind rows behind rows. They were very long, but when I stepped out of line, I could see both ends. I stood next to my mother.

Once everybody was standing in order, we waited, but nothing happened. Finally, the barracks elder appeared with a young soldier and started to count. They did not ask our names. We had become only numbers.

When they had finished, we thought we could go, but we were ordered back into line.

They counted us again.

And again.

Obviously, the numbers didn't add up.

The barracks elder went inside, and after a while he reappeared, dragging a half-dead woman with the help of another inmate. The woman stumbled, but no one really seemed to care about her. It was a horrible sight and my mum turned my head away.

Now, at last, the numbers were correct, and we could go back to the barracks.

This procedure, Mum told me, was called the roll call or *Appell* in German, and the place we were ordered to stand was called the *Appellplatz*. We did not know the first time, but the roll calls became the dominant part of our daily life. They were held every morning, but occasionally also in the afternoon for a second time, and they lasted for ever.

The numbers never added up and the counts had to be repeated. Again and again. Some people were too weak to leave the barracks or were sick or had died.

But the most horrible thing was when the guards found the bodies of the missing people on the barbed wire of the fence. My dad explained that it had electricity running through it. I was told never even to approach it. Dad also told me – what I had already guessed – that these unfortunate people had taken their own lives.

What I saw later was worse. Much worse. And my mother could not turn my head away, because the horror by that time was all around me.

To make the roll calls even longer, there were endless intervals between each count. It was my most dreaded part of the day. The cold was hardly bearable: the freezing temperature was made much worse by razor-sharp winds. The chill penetrated my body, starting at my feet, as my shoes and socks weren't warm enough. After the meagre breakfast, I soon got hungry. Hunger had become part of our day – our most loyal companion, which never left us.

But, for me, it was not the cold or the hunger but the boredom that was the worst. Standing in lines for hours and not being able to do anything. I could not leave the line and was hardly able to move. Mum told me to move my arms and legs as much as possible, to jump up and down without drawing the attention of the guards. But, still, the boredom was overwhelming.

Then, one day, my mother came up with an idea: "Why don't I start to teach you? In happier times you would be in school soon. So, if you're so bored, why don't we start with numbers?"

"But I know the numbers: one, two, three, four, five, six, seven, eight, nine, ten... I can carry on..."

"All right. But let's add up. Three plus four?"

I was baffled, but then I put up three fingers on one hand and four on the other and made a quick count: "Seven."

"Correct. Now: seven plus six?"

I couldn't answer, but I knew that I didn't have enough fingers to add this up.

"All right, don't worry," said Mum. "We're going to learn."

So we did. Adding up first, then subtracting, multiplying and dividing. I cannot say that time exactly flew, but I was certainly not bored. These exercises stood me in good stead later at school and perhaps sowed the seed of my aptitude for mathematics.

To add some variation to my education, my mum later started to teach me German. I found this rather strange.

"Aren't the Germans our enemy? Don't we hate them?"

"Yes, the Germans are our enemy, but we don't hate them – only those who want to kill us. We don't hate their language. Some of the greatest work in literature was written in German."

When we met up with my father, Mum told him that his son was learning German. He was not happy at all.

"Are you mad? You're teaching our son the language of people who are intent on killing us."

But Mum did not give in: "First, don't call me mad. Second, don't talk about killing in front of Peter. And don't forget, people spoke this language for centuries before these madmen arrived. And people will speak it long after the Nazis have disappeared."

"All right."

Dad gave in, and my German lessons continued.

By lunchtime, we were ravenously hungry. We lined up inside the barracks, and one of the women started to ladle the food out. For the first time in my life, I was not sure what I was eating. It didn't taste of anything much, but since it was warm, I started to spoon it into my mouth. It was a thin soup with pieces of unrecognizable vegetables in it – a far cry from those my mother used to make: like chicken soup all year round and pea soup in the summer.

"What are we eating?"

"It's a sort of soup with vegetables," Mum said.

"It is not. It isn't the vegetable soup you used to make."

"When we had vegetable soup, you didn't like it."

"It wasn't as good as the chicken soup."

"Well, whatever it is, you've got to eat it. There is nothing else."

"I don't know what this is," I complained as I fished out a tasteless piece of vegetable.

"I think it's turnip."

I fished out another piece, which was pale pink, and held it up to Mum.

"It must have been beetroot once."

We later learned that the name of this soup was *Dörrgemüse*, and it became our everyday food for lunch. It varied little, and we were very fortunate when the liquid contained some potatoes. On these occasions the distribution was carefully monitored so that no one should get away with more pieces of potato than others.

Occasionally, when the woman who ladled out the soup looked up and saw it was a child holding out the tin plate, she turned the soup with the ladle to find a potato and put it on my plate. Mum thanked her for her kindness.

For dinner we got bread, occasionally with a little butter or a slice of cheese or sausage.

The greatest feast was when we received additional food, sent by the Red Cross. When I asked Mum, she explained that the Red Cross was an international organization trying to help people like us. When I asked why they didn't give us food all the time, she said it was not possible, but she didn't say why.

These better meals were unfortunately rather rare, but the taste of biscuits, meat and good jam and marmalade brought back memories of a time when hunger was unknown to us.

However, the most precious food was bread. It was rationed, and the amount gradually decreased during our stay. From early spring, we occasionally received more than one day's portion at a time, which some people ate straight away. It was so tempting to eat the whole lot immediately, but I soon had to learn that all my protests and begging were completely in vain. Mum told me that I would starve to death if I ate all the bread in one go. She was strict and never gave me more than I should have for the day, though sometimes she gave me a bit of hers.

Yet even with the additional bread I was hungry most of the time.

The greatest crime was stealing someone else's bread. Mum guarded our portion as if it were gold. When we were not in the barracks, she took it with her.

It seemed that winter would never end. The freezing temperatures were made much worse by bitterly cold winds. Standing at roll calls became unbearable. Even my mum's private lessons did not make the endless waiting much better. Yet, when snow fell, I was quite happy.

I tried to make snowmen behind the barracks with the other children, and we fought battles with freshly made snowballs when the guards could not see us. There was another reason why I felt better when the snow arrived. If it fell for long enough and the wind did not blow it away, a white blanket covered the ground and even this ugly place looked so much better. It also covered the dead.

The long winter came to a slow and reluctant end, and finally spring arrived.

It was now a pleasure to get out of the barracks into the

open air. Since there were no trees near the barracks, Mum suggested that we visit a small copse to see the first buds, which were just beginning to unfurl. This would be an adventure. After *Appel*, on a day when the sky was blue and the sun shone, we went to see the trees. After the barren, frozen ground it was so beautiful to see real trees with the green shoots of life.

I wished that Zsuzsi and Aunt Anna were there.

It was at this time that I started to notice that there were many more people around. When I pointed this out to Mum, she said, "Yes, there are. And they keep coming."

"Where from?

"From the east."

"Where is east?"

"Where the sun rises."

I found this answer unsatisfactory: "Which country? Hungary?"

"They're from Poland and Russia."

"How do you know?"

"I asked them. Many are from Hungary too. They're coming from camps like ours."

Now, I thought of Zsuzsi and Aunt Anna again. The last time I had seen them had been in Szeged when they got on the other train: "Do you think that Aunt Anna and Zsuzsi might be in one of these camps in the east?"

"I don't know. I wish I did."

"Why didn't these people who keep arriving stay where they were?"

For a second, I thought that Mum would tell me to shut up, but she didn't.

"They couldn't because the Russian Army is liberating places the Germans previously occupied, so the prisoners are being transferred before they can be freed."

"Will the Russians liberate us too?"

"Not very likely. They're far away from us. If anybody is going to liberate us, it will be the British or the Americans."

"Does this mean that the Germans are losing the war?"

"Yes. I think you've asked enough questions for today."

I knew that now I really should shut up. During the last few months, after my dad had been separated from us, I had to spend all my time with Mum. I felt much closer to her – like she was not only my mother, but also an old friend. Like Gyuri, my brother.

Of course, I kept these thoughts to myself. I knew that I could ask any questions I wanted, yet I learned where the boundaries were which I shouldn't cross. My mother also maintained a strict discipline which, I didn't realize at the time, saved my life – more than once.

*

With spring, something else – most unwelcome – arrived. It was death. People had been dying since the day we arrived, but not in such large numbers as in the spring. Those who died earlier were usually cremated. I remembered the building with the tall, odd-looking chimney we had discovered during our tour on the first day. It was a crematorium where they burned dead people.

However, despite the cremations, there seemed to be more and more bodies lying around. I didn't understand why. The camp became very crowded with the new arrivals, and they must have brought death with them.

"They die of infection and starvation," Mum told me.

"I know what infections are, but what's starvation?"

"When you don't have enough food for a long time, and you become so weak that life stops." Suddenly I understood why so many of the dead people looked so terrible. They consisted of only bones and skin, and their faces looked like those skulls you see on warning signs about danger of death.

"But *we* don't have enough food…"

Mum interrupted: "While you can keep asking questions, you're not going to die of starvation. When you stop asking, then I'll start worrying." I looked at her, and for the first time in a long while I saw her smiling.

Just to prove that I wasn't yet dying of starvation, I asked, "What sort of infections?"

"Well, one of the doctors in the 'hospital' is Hungarian. He told me that there are a whole range of infections. Typhus…"

"What's that?"

"If you'd stop interrupting, I'll tell you. Remember we had lice? They carry a bug that causes typhus, which then spreads."

"How do you know you have typhus?"

"You have a high temperature and terrible runny tummy. We will certainly know if we get it. I pray to God we don't."

"What are the others?" I asked.

"Shall we change the subject?" Mum replied.

"But I want to know!"

"Do you think you should know everything?"

"Yes."

"Typhoid fever, dysentery and tuberculosis. The first two are diseases of your stomach and gut, the last is an infectious disease of the lungs. Now you know."

"I hope we aren't going to get them," I said, not daring to ask anything further.

"So do I. So do I."

We met my dad regularly. Mum and I went to see him, or he came to visit us. These meetings always happened in the open air, however freezing it was. My mum could not enter the men's barracks, nor could Dad come inside ours. The meetings were short. They usually started with Dad asking how I was, then my parents talked to each other.

Occasionally I noticed Mum giving something to Dad, usually at a moment when she thought I couldn't see. After one such visit I asked what it was.

"It's none of your business," she said. I was surprised by this reply since she was usually very good at answering my questions. Then she changed her mind: "All right, if you have to know, it's bread."

I was so surprised that I couldn't speak for a moment: "You're not going to give our bread away...?"

"Don't you worry, it's not *our* bread."

"Are you stealing...?"

"You don't think that I would steal other starving people's bread, do you?" Somehow, I immediately knew that I was wrong. Would Mum commit the greatest crime of the camp?

"I'm sorry."

"I'm *not* stealing other people's bread. I'm working for it."

"Working for it? How?"

"It's still none of your business, but if you want to know ... I wash other people's dirty clothes for an extra slice. And give it to Dad."

Now it made sense. Mum always seemed to stay for a long time in the "bathroom" after she had sent me back to the barracks.

"But Dad also has his ration, doesn't he?"

"Yes, he does. But where do you think your dad gets his cigarettes?" This was yet another of Mum's tricks: never giving away the answer, but making me think so I arrived at the right answer myself.

I knew Dad was a heavy smoker. Cigarettes were never far from him. My most memorable picture of him was him reading the paper and smoking a cigarette. On one occasion he fell asleep with the cigarette in his mouth, and a spark fell on the paper and started a fire. This led to a quarrel and a small victory for Mum: "Do you want to burn the house down?"

After this incident, Dad agreed not to smoke in bed. However, he didn't give up smoking altogether. When he came to say goodnight in the evening, I could smell the strong scent of tobacco.

"He must be buying them."

There were no shops in the camp and, anyway, Dad

didn't have any money. So how did he get his cigarettes?

Suddenly it dawned on me. "He sells his bread for cigarettes?"

"Correct. There is a small black market where people trade the little they have, and your dad exchanges his bread for cigarettes."

"But if he does that, he'll die!"

"Try telling him. Or rather, don't, since he'll be very angry. I've told him many times, but it's no use. I'm afraid that even the extra portions I bring him from time to time might be exchanged."

She saw that I was so surprised and confused that I couldn't even ask a question, which wasn't like me at all.

"This should remain between us; it's our secret. Understand?"

I nodded.

Towards the end of February, Dad's visits stopped, and it was always Mum and me who went to see him. He would come out of his barracks to greet us, but he was so weak that eventually there came a time that another man from the same barracks had to bring him out.

He could hardly stand on his own feet. We exchanged a couple of the usual sentences. His voice was so weak that I barely understood what he said.

When we were about to leave, he put his hand on my head without saying a word, as if he were blessing me.

As we were about to turn the corner, I looked back from the end of the path in front of his barracks, but by then he had disappeared.

That was the last time we saw him alive.

A couple of days later, a man came and asked for Mum. I was slow to follow her outside and couldn't hear what the man said, but I could hear Mum clearly:

"Has he died?"

The man said nothing, looking at me, and nodded.

"Where is he now?"

"In the 'hospital'."

I remembered this was the place where Mum was taken on the day we arrived, after she was beaten.

"Thank you for letting us know. We'll be there in a few minutes."

We returned to the barracks, and Mum gave me my overcoat and put on hers since it was still cold on that March morning. She didn't cry.

We walked through the camp to the hospital. Inside, a man, as old as Dad, came towards us. He introduced himself in Hungarian. He said he was a doctor, but I did not catch his name.

"I treated your husband. I'm sorry, but I couldn't save him."

"Thank you anyway," said Mum.

"You came to see him?"

"Yes, and this is my son, Peter. Where is he?"

We were led to a bed. Dad was there: even thinner than when we had seen him the last time. His skin was a yellowish colour. I should have cried, but I couldn't. I just wanted to get out of there.

"What did he die of?" asked Mum – also still not crying.

"Enteritis, inflammation of the intestines, complicated by heart problems."

I did not understand any of this.

"But he didn't have heart disease at home," Mum said.

"Obviously I couldn't investigate it here, since we don't have any equipment, as I'm sure you must know. However, it was probably malnutrition, which eventually led to the breakdown of his bodily systems. If you want, I can show you: I recorded it, unofficially, in a booklet. Your husband might be the last entry, since so many people die every day that I cannot keep up with the records. Many don't even reach the hospital and die in their barracks."

With this, the doctor handed a small, well-used booklet

to Mum, who quickly looked at it and passed it back to him.

"Thank you."

I looked at Mum and saw that now she was crying.

She noticed that I was watching her and pulled me close. I was so lost that I still couldn't cry – and didn't until much later.

"What will happen now?" Mum asked.

This was the first time that I had seen her helpless.

"You should ask the men from his barracks to come and say the prayer for the dead, but I don't know what will be done afterwards. As you can see, all around us so many people are dying that we can't do anything about them all. I know this must be very upsetting for you."

"I do understand. Can I do anything?"

"I'm afraid you can't. He might be cremated; that would be the best. The worst is that his body might be left unburied. I'm sorry for not being able to do more."

Later we went back to the hospital, where a few men were gathering around the bed in which Dad lay. The prayer was said, as the kind doctor had instructed. Mum and I joined the men.

But we never knew what happened to my dad's body. He was prisoner 8432.

As we were walking back to the barracks, Mum said,

"Your father died at eight in the morning. Just a couple of hours ago. I saw the date of death in the doctor's book: the thirteenth of March. We arrived on the seventh of December: so we've been here just over four months."

"It seems much longer."

"Yes, it does. Worse still, we don't know for how much longer we'll have to stay. Or even if we'll survive."

Later in the spring – by then it must have been April – after countless *Appels* and countless meals of bread and water, Mum told me that people were saying that the British Army was nearby and they were going to liberate us. Planes were overflying quite low and more and more frequently than in previous months. When I looked up, I could see that they did not have the frightening black cross on them, but coloured circles of blue, white and red.

At first, we were terrified that they were going to bomb us, but they left after descending low over the camp – so low that on one occasion I could see the pilot. Mum told me that they were British planes and they flew over us to see what was going on here.

Mum solved the mystery: "They are flying to see the layout of the camp. For the army when it arrives."

Another good sign that the end was near was the fact

that many of the hated SS guards had disappeared. When we arrived, they had seemed to be everywhere on the ground. You could hear them around every corner, but, most threateningly, see them in the watchtowers. Whenever I had to walk near one of those, I looked up to check where they were looking – very carefully, so that they would not notice me. However, they hardly ever entered the barracks, so it felt a bit safer in there. Mum said they did not want to get any diseases.

"The rats are leaving the sinking ship," Mum commented now, once we were safely in our bunk, snuggled next to each other.

At the same time more and more people were dying and the ground was covered by the dead: singly or in groups, sometimes dozens on top of each other. When we walked out, as she always did, Mum tried to turn my head away so that I didn't see too much, but later the bodies were everywhere. I was frightened, but at the same time I wanted to see; I don't know why. Mum couldn't completely hide the picture: bodies lying on the barren ground. They were so thin that they didn't really look like real people. I thought their arms and legs looked like twigs and it was so sad to see them all jumbled together in piles. Some of them didn't even have any clothes.

The worst was to have them in the barracks, since no one took them away and we had to try to pass them every day without looking too closely.

Bread rations became even smaller and there was a water shortage. We could not wash ourselves in the "bathroom" and we became increasingly dirty.

We prayed for the British to come but they did not. We thought we were going to die in the camp.

Then one day something unexpected happened.

There was a meeting in the barracks and Mum came back very excited.

"We must pack. We are leaving."

While I understood what she had said, I didn't know what it meant. "Leaving?"

"Yes, we are leaving Belsen."

"But we can't. We're prisoners."

"Could you not argue, just for once? We are leaving. The barracks elder has just announced that the Germans are organizing three trains to leave the camp. Each will carry about two and half thousand people."

"But there must be many more in the camp. I heard someone saying—"

"Yes, there are. But the camp won't be emptied or closed. Only a small percentage of the prisoners can leave. I volunteered to go."

"But where are we going?"

This question seemed to weaken my mother's resolve. "I don't know. But anywhere is better than here. We must go and pack immediately."

Packing didn't take long, since, by then, there was practically nothing to take. We hadn't got anything.

"What about food?"

"We might get some for the journey. Or we might not. But whatever happens we must go."

It was a clear April day when we left the camp. My mother told me later that it was 6 April. The British liberated the camp on 15 April.

Chapter 7

Destination unknown

All the comforts of our world were now reduced to a bag. As we were leaving, we saw that many people from other barracks were joining us, carrying their equally small amount of luggage. We were ordered to line up. Unexpectedly, I was happy, since I hoped that this was the last roll call.

After all, we were going to leave this hell.

Our names were read and ticked off on a long list. It was then we finally realized that there were thousands of people going to the station. We formed a marching column, and the barrier of the camp was lifted for us to leave.

We did not look back.

We were back on the road we had marched along the previous December.

Despite the milder weather, the march did not seem to be

any shorter than the first time we had walked from the train station to the camp. Weakened by months of starvation, I got increasingly tired. I thought we would never arrive. Clutching my mum's hand, I kept asking her how long we had to walk.

"We'll get there soon. Keep walking," she said.

"Can we stop?"

"No, we can't.

"Why not?"

Silently, she pointed to the soldier: "We must go on."

"Where are we going?"

"To the station," she said. And, as a first sign that she was getting tired of my enquiries, she added, "How many times do I have to tell you? To the station."

"How far is the station?"

"Six kilometres from where we started. We must have walked more than three by now. It's not all that far."

"But we have been walking for hours."

"No, we haven't. We've been walking for less than an hour. We'll soon be there."

"I'm getting very tired."

"I know, but we must go on."

"I want to sit down."

"No, you can't. We can't stop. You understand?" She

looked at me without stopping, to see signs of whether I was going to start to cry or throw a tantrum.

I decided against both actions and kept on walking.

"Instead of looking at the backs of the people marching in front of you," Mum said, "why don't you look around? What can you see?"

I followed her advice and saw well-kept houses standing in the middle of tidy gardens. It all looked different from when we had seen it in December: the snow had disappeared and the houses and gardens had regained their colours in the sunshine. In one of the gardens there was a grey horse. It was a picture I thought I would never see again: houses and gardens and flowers – images which had been erased from my sight for such a long time. And now there was even a horse in one of the gardens we had passed!

It reminded me of the time when one of the workers in the timber yard, under my mum's watchful eyes, lifted me up and put me on the back of a small pony.

I looked at the gardens again. It was early April, but some of the trees already had green leaves. I was happy seeing the signs of spring and the end of the freezing days and the even colder nights. In the flower beds there were beautiful white, pink, purple and blue blooms.

"What are they?" I pointed at them.

"Hyacinths. Don't you remember? We used to have them at home." Even before she had finished the sentence, she realized that she had said the wrong thing. It was home I wanted to be more than anywhere else.

"When are we going to get home?"

"I don't know."

"If we are going to the station, the train might take us home."

"It might, but I doubt it."

"So where will the train take us?"

"I don't know. Believe me, if I knew, I'd tell you. Promise."

This was a further confirmation of the bond which had been growing between us since my father's death. I felt proud that she took me seriously.

She continued: "I asked one of the guards and he didn't know. That's what he told me, anyway. No one seems to know. When we reach the station, we may find out."

We kept marching. There were lines and lines of us, masses of people, hundreds and hundreds, marching in undulating lines, sometimes slowing down, then regaining some speed, bullied by the guards: "Fast, fast; faster, faster," they shouted, occasionally using truncheons on those who were particularly slow.

I saw a couple of people falling to the ground, but we could not stop.

Exhausted and with my feet hurting, we finally arrived at the station. I looked up and could read the sign. It said:

BERGEN

At first, it didn't mean anything. Then with a sudden flash, I remembered that this was the station we had arrived at exactly four months earlier on an ice-cold day in December. We had not known where we were or how long we were going to stay or what was waiting for us in this place in Germany. But soon enough we had found out.

Now, once again, we did not know where we were going. But I remembered that my mother had said that anywhere would be better than in Belsen.

This promise kept me going, and surveying the train cheered me up. It was a mixture of ordinary-looking passenger carriages and cattle wagons. The presence of the "normal" carriages made this train different from all the others we had travelled in since we left Hungary. But who was going to travel in the carriages and who would be in the cattle wagons?

The train was also very long, and I stopped counting at twenty: there were more cattle wagons than carriages. I noticed that behind the train's engine there was an open wagon from which a large gun and other smaller guns pointed towards the sky.

My mum noticed this too. "It isn't a very good sign," she muttered.

"Why?"

"*Why?* Guns are not for a peaceful journey."

A further bad sign was the appearance of SS guards from the camp. In this long train there was only one first-class car, just behind the wagon with the guns. I would have loved to travel in it after having so many terrible journeys in cattle wagons. However, my hope did not last long as I saw the SS getting into it.

"We were prisoners in the camps and we remain prisoners on the train," Mum said.

The scuffles and chaos which broke out to get into the carriages were stopped by a loud order. Those with small children were given priority. My mum and I were lucky – we got into a small compartment which soon became very crowded. We could sit, but there was no question of lying down for the night.

Before we got on to the train, we were given some food: bread, cheese, pieces of sausage and jam. It was quite exciting to get a bit of sausage.

For a long time, nothing happened.

We waited for the train to pull out of the station, but it remained stationary. We lowered the window of the compartment to get some fresh air. The evening turned into night, but the train still did not move. I must have fallen asleep with my head in Mum's lap.

It was morning when I woke up. Later we had a small slice of bread and an even smaller piece of cheese. In the afternoon, the train slowly started to move, just to stop after a few minutes.

It wasn't until the next morning when the train finally pulled out of the station. In the meantime, Mum had found out that we might be travelling to another concentration camp called Theresienstadt.

"Where is Theresienstadt?" I asked Mum.

"I don't know exactly, but it's near Prague."

"Where is Prague?"

"It's a very long way away. It was once the capital of a country called Czechoslovakia. Now it's part of the German Empire."

"And how long will it take to get there?"

"I don't know. If the train goes at this snail's pace and doesn't speed up, it will take a very long time."

Even I noticed how slow the train was. I spent the

time pressing my nose to the window and watching the countryside. We passed through many forests and some open fields and old towns and villages.

When the train stopped again, we were allowed to get off and look for water. As we were walking next to the tracks we could see through the open doors of the cattle wagons: they were very crowded, just like those we had travelled in previously. How lucky we had been to get into a carriage. We were also given bread and some yellow creamy stuff that turned out to be margarine, not butter, but it tasted good.

The second day I noticed that one of the luggage racks was empty. With Mum's help I climbed up to sleep. During the night there was an air raid, and my mum told me that the train might be a target for Allied bombing.

At first, I could only hear a sort of buzzing, but quite quickly the noise became much louder. It felt as if the planes were going right over the top of us and I wanted to cover my head with my arms. I put my hands over my ears and closed my eyes, waiting for it to be over. The planes were flying quite low, and the German soldiers must have used the guns we had seen when we had got on the train. There was a gun very close to our carriage and it made the windows shake.

However, the planes left so soon that we did not even have time to get off the train.

"Why would they bomb us? We aren't the enemy."

"The pilots can see the gun and might think that our train is carrying German soldiers."

She was right. Next day we had another air raid. This was more dangerous than the previous one. We heard explosions nearby and the train stopped. Someone must have opened the door of the carriage and we left the train as fast as we could. The explosions became louder and louder. Mum did not waste time: "Lie down," she said, and we both lay down on the grass next to the tracks. Many people were doing the same, and only a few remained in our carriage. As we heard more explosions, Mum said, "Listen carefully. If anything happens to me—"

"What would happen to you?" I interrupted, since I knew what she was going to say and didn't want to hear it.

"Don't interrupt me. If I die, you must make sure that you know enough information about yourself to be identified. You know your name, date of birth and the name of the town where we live." I nodded.

"Do you know my name?"

"Yes."

"Say it."

"Mrs…"

"Not my married name. My maiden name. My name before I married your father."

"Ilona Schwartz." As I said her name, I suddenly asked myself the most horrible question: what would I do in the world without her? I wanted to cry out, but I remained silent.

"Clever boy. Your dad's surname?"

"That's easy. It's the same as mine. But his name is Sándor and not Peter."

"Do you remember our address?"

"Yes, I do," I said, and recited it.

"Good. Well done." Then she turned to a woman lying next to her in the grass, who had been in our compartment: "You remember my son?

"Yes, I do."

"If anything happens to me, please look after him. He knows…"

I turned away, since I did not want to hear the rest.

We got back on to the train, which stopped again after a short time. We noticed that some of the SS guards were leaving the train. We were in a town and we could see that it had been heavily bombed, since there were many ruins next to the railway tracks. There were lots of people rushing about, carrying large suitcases and pushing carts. Others were crowded into cars. They were Germans and they seemed to be escaping. There was panic and we didn't know why.

We soon learned what was going on. The Germans near the train shouted something in our direction which I did not understand. My mum translated: "They are warning us not to go any further. There are American soldiers nearby."

"God bless them; that's exactly where we want to go," shouted someone in the compartment.

The train started again, just to stop on the open track in the middle of nowhere. The track was bordered on either side by slopes dotted with trees. I looked out, but there was nobody around.

There was silence. A long silence.

Suddenly we heard rumbling, which gradually intensified. I didn't know what it was, but I thought it might be tanks.

The Germans were coming back!

A woman in the compartment shouted, "That's the end! We're all going to die!"

But she was wrong. For it was the beginning...

Chapter 8

The first days of freedom

The rumbling became ear-splitting, but then it suddenly stopped. There was silence again. I heard the doors of the wagons being opened and someone shouted at the top of her voice, "It's the Americans! The Americans have arrived!"

We opened the door of our carriage and I did not wait for my mother to help me down, but jumped and started to run towards the front of the train. Mum caught up with me and, grabbing my hand, she also started to run.

On the track, in front of the train's engine, soldiers were climbing out of two tanks. They were so different from the people who had surrounded us in the camp. They were tall and well fed and clean and did not wear the hated uniform of the SS guards.

My mother confirmed: "They're Americans. We *are* free." I looked at her and saw that she was silently crying:

tears rolling down her face. "It's terrible that your father is not with us," she said.

We were surrounded by more and more people from the train. We saw that the American soldiers had arrested a few guards: those who had not escaped earlier. I saw a young woman who must have been on the train talking to one of the American soldiers, who, as we learned later, was commander of one of the tanks.

She translated from English into German what the officer told her. And Mum translated it into Hungarian for me. "He was saying that we're now free! They're part of a much larger tank battalion and they'll look after us for the night. They didn't know what the train was carrying and couldn't believe that people could be treated like we were." Mum stopped and tried not to cry.

"What else did the tank commander say?"

"If you stop interrupting, I'll tell you. They don't have any food yet for so many people and they don't know where we're going to sleep, but they'll try to get some food from the village over there. We must be patient – there might not be enough for everyone. And they're also looking to find somewhere for us to sleep tonight…"

One of the officers had a camera and started to take pictures: of the train, the people around him, a guard with his hands up in the air, surrendering. He asked the children to form a group to be photographed and I was happy to join in. My mother did not share my enthusiasm. Since we had been in the camp, she hadn't wanted me to leave her side, even by a couple of metres. She watched from nearby and did not move until I ran back to her.

Some of the people lined up and it looked like they were introducing themselves to the Americans. My mum was reluctant at first, but at my nagging we joined the queue and introduced ourselves. I was surprised when she said, "Thank you," in English.

"I didn't know that you also speak English."

"I don't. But I saw enough American films before the war to pick up a couple of words."

However, she did not want to waste more time, since there was something she was determined to do: "We must try to clean ourselves up," she said.

Even I had to agree, since we were dirty from the long train journey. We found what I thought was a stream, but it could have been only a ditch. We washed ourselves, but the water was very cold. Despite my initial protests, I felt much better afterwards.

Mum found out that it was 13 April. She said we must have been on the train for six days.

We still had no idea exactly where we were, until the lady who had talked to the Americans told everyone that we were near a village called Farsleben and the nearest city was Magdeburg. Of course, I didn't know where that was, but my mother told me that we were still in Germany and very far from Prague.

It was early spring, and the days were short. The temperature suddenly dropped as the sun disappeared. I was cold and hungry. We didn't know what was going to happen. Should we go back to the train? Wait for further instructions?

In the end we didn't have to wait too long. The Americans hadn't wasted any time. They had managed to arrange for many people from the train to stay in the village.

At first Mum was reluctant to enter a German house, but this is how we spent our first night of freedom.

And the next day everything changed.

On our first day of real freedom, the Americans got military vehicles and some civilian buses and we were transferred to a beautiful place. It was near a village called Hillersleben. As we passed it, we could see houses and the tall spire of a church. Our new home was on a modern estate, built for German officers and their families, we were told.

The houses were two or three floors high. Most of their inhabitants were told to leave to give us space. By the time we got there, the majority of them had already left, but we saw a few people carrying their luggage. Seeing them reminded me of the time when we had to leave our house. However, it was my mother who said what I was thinking: "Now they know what it's like when one is forced to leave one's home."

The streets were lined with trees and in a square there was a children's playground. I hadn't seen anything like it since we had left Hungary.

Before we were allowed to go inside the houses, we had to go through a process of disinfection.

"Not again," I protested.

We were taken to what must have been the local hospital. This was very different from the place in the camp where we had been disinfected, as was our treatment.

Here, it was very clean and the whole place smelled of what Mum told me was disinfectant. The American soldiers seemed to be in charge. We waited outside a large room. When we entered, I saw several cubicles, and each seemed to be curtained off. Mum and I went into one and a nurse told us to undress. Here, there was no shortage of the stuff we were sprayed with and there was plenty of hot water and soap afterwards. People in white gowns made sure that we didn't have lice anymore. We also had to register, which by now had become a familiar procedure.

Finally, my mum and I were allocated a nice room on the first floor of a modern building. It was beautifully furnished. There was a large bed with bedside tables on either side, quite similar to the ones we had at home. A table, two armchairs and a large wardrobe completed the furnishings. It was so good to see a proper bed with a plump mattress after so long and I wanted to get in and sleep straight away! It looked truly wonderful.

"If it was good enough for German officers and their families it should be good enough for us," said Mum as we looked around the room. After six months this was a new life.

And we had food!

Food like we had not had for months. It seemed that the families of the German officers had not suffered from starvation. In the kitchen we found fat sausages, jars of colourful jams, large pieces of delicious cheese and tins of things I couldn't even recognize because the labels were in German.

In addition, soon after our arrival in Hillersleben, the Americans *also* gave us food – and there was no shortage! Mum told me that they organized everything, making sure that everybody could eat. Communal meals were organized in a large building which, according to Mum, used to be a casino (whatever that was). In the very same building, we saw many American soldiers eating in a large hall. Food, both fresh and tinned, was distributed daily. Bread was baked daily. And the Americans also distributed more tinned food: mainly meat, some of which I did not recognize, but it tasted delicious.

My mother was also very enterprising. As spring turned into summer, we collected fresh fruit from some of the gardens. When this was ripe, we ate it straight away after washing it in our flat, but if it was still hard she cooked it to make delicious stewed fruit, adding a little sugar.

I could have eaten all day to make up for months of hunger. I could have ... but Mum wouldn't allow me to. She strictly rationed what and how much and when I could eat. We ate often but only in very small amounts.

I was confused about why Mum wouldn't let me eat more food when we had plenty.

"For months we have not eaten properly," she explained. "We have had bad food, which didn't have any proper nourishment in it. Your body is not accustomed to the food we have now. Your digestion cannot cope with it. Do you understand?"

I had a vague idea what she was saying, but I said, "No, I don't. Haven't we starved for long enough?"

"Yes, we have. But you don't want to die now, do you?"

I didn't know why I would die from satisfying my hunger, but I reluctantly agreed to do as she said. She gradually increased the portions, and within a week I wasn't hungry anymore.

Mum told me that a girl who was staying in the same house as us had died because she ate too much. At first, I didn't believe her, but then I realized I hadn't seen the girl for a while and decided it must be true.

She was the daughter of the family who were living in the room next door. I'd met them soon after we arrived. The parents were younger than my mum and their daughter was my age, maybe a little bit older. She had blonde hair and was even thinner than I was. A couple of days later I could hear shouting and crying from their room and I thought that they were having an argument.

When I asked what had happened, Mum confirmed that it was the day when the little girl had fallen ill and been taken to hospital, where she had died.

Slowly we tried to get back to normal life. In the mornings we washed ourselves in the bathroom with hot water and soap. This was a great luxury after the camp. Then we had breakfast in the kitchen, which we shared with three other families, enjoying proper coffee with milk.

After breakfast I would go to play with other children; most of the time my mum came with me. Then we'd go back to the flat to have lunch. To gain my strength back, I often snoozed in the afternoons.

When I woke up, my mum would continue her teaching: this time it was learning to read and write. She explained, "At home, you would go to school in September, but we may not get back in time."

The highlight of my day was when a regular visitor came to see us. At dusk on our first evening in Hillersleben, there had been a knock on our door. Before we could open it, a man walked into our room. He was very tall – the top of his head reached the doorframe – but what surprised me most was the colour of his skin. Until that moment, I had never seen a Black man before. Later I would meet many Black soldiers, all in the uniform of the American Army, but at that point, I had never seen anyone like him. He stopped in the door and said, "Good evening."

Mum understood those two words, but not the rest of what the soldier was saying. We did not even know why he had come. However, what he did next clearly explained the purpose of his visit, without further words. He walked to the window and closed the shutters. Since this was our first night in the flat, we hadn't even known that there *were* shutters. When he had finished, he said, "Goodbye," and left.

I was excited and hoped that he would come again.

The second evening, he returned at the same time. Again, he said, "Good evening." Then he turned around to survey the room and spotted me. He smiled and fished out a bar wrapped in shiny foil from his pocket, then handed it to me.

"Chocolate. It's for you."

I understood the first word, since it sounded very similar in Hungarian. I hesitated.

"Accept it and say thank you," said my mum.

I thanked him in Hungarian and then in German.

He laughed and said, "*Thank you.*"

"*Thank you,*" I repeated, and without any further hesitation I tore off the foil and bit off half of the chocolate. It was delicious and brought back distant memories of home. This was how our friendship started.

During the third visit he introduced himself.

"My name is Henry," he said, pointing at himself. Even without the gesture, I would have understood.

"My name is Ilona," Mum said. "And my son is Peter."

"My name is Peter," I repeated with pride at my newly acquired English knowledge.

The soldier sat down and produced a wallet. He opened it and showed a picture to Mum and then to me.

It was a photograph of a woman and a small boy. He pointed at the boy and at me.

My mother also produced a photograph of the four of us, which she had managed to keep throughout the journey. It was taken by one of my uncles before we were deported. I listened hard but did not understand the exchange of words that followed between them.

The soldier did not speak German and Mum did not speak English. However, they seemed to have understood each other. After he left, she explained that the woman in the photo was his wife and the boy was his son. His son was my age and going to school in the autumn. Mum had told him that the man in our photo was her husband and the older boy was my brother.

He returned every evening to check whether the shutters were closed. The war was still going on and there was still a danger that German planes might bomb us. After dark, the brightly lit windows of houses, like ours, might help the enemy to find their targets.

During blackouts, streetlights had to be switched off and windows covered.

Our regular daily life was soon upset by an unexpected event.

I had an accident.

After my nap in the afternoon, I was allowed to go down and play with the other children. The streets were safe, with hardly any traffic. Mum trusted me to keep out of trouble. Usually, we went to the nearby children's playground. This had poles to climb, a small sandpit surrounded by wooden planks, a couple of see-saws and swings.

One afternoon on the way to the playground, I was kicking a ball around on the pavement with a couple of other boys. Soon we extended the game to the road, since the ball often rolled away. I was running to recover the ball from the road and didn't notice a jeep turning the corner.

I do not know what happened next, but I heard my playmates screaming and the repeated hooting of the jeep. Suddenly, I felt an intense pain in my back and everything went black.

When I saw light again, I was lying on the road. I looked up and I saw several faces peering down at me: Mum's, a few American soldiers' and two of the boys'. I had never been the centre of so much attention. My mother lifted me up, and as she did I could see blood on the road. It must have been mine.

The driver helped her, as she carried me in her arms to the jeep. He drove us to the local hospital. I was examined by a doctor and had an X-ray.

Despite the blood, fortunately it was a minor accident. The mudguard of the jeep had torn the skin of my back, but the wound was superficial and nothing in my body was broken. They kept us in the hospital for a couple of hours. One of the doctors told my mum in German that if I had any problems during the night we should come back immediately. Then we were driven home.

"Are you all right?" Mum asked.

I did not dare to say anything, just nodded. My back still ached very badly.

"You could have been killed. Don't ever do that again."

I wasn't sure how Mum had found out I'd been hurt, but it turned out one of the boys I was playing with knew where we lived and had rushed up to tell her what had happened. His name was Tibi and he lived with his family in the block next door. We'd visited each other a few times and I'd met his parents. His father was a lawyer in Szeged. He also had a teenage brother whom I did not like: he was not very friendly.

Since the accident happened just around the corner from where we lived, my mum had run as fast as she could and arrived a couple of minutes after the car had hit me. She hadn't even had time to put a proper dress on and had rushed out in a dressing gown she'd found in the wardrobe along with some dresses that had belonged to the German officer's wife who'd lived there before us.

When she saw me in a pool of blood, surrounded by people, she feared the worst. As she lifted me, her dressing gown became soaked with blood, but she realized that I was alive.

Later that same evening, the driver of the jeep arrived with a translator to apologize. He explained that he had not been driving fast, but hadn't seen me as he turned the corner. As a peace offering, he brought a large bar of chocolate.

I paid a heavy price for my accident. From that day on, my mother never allowed me to go to the playground on my own; she always came with me. All my protests were in vain.

Soon after we had moved into the flat, Mum found a diary. From that time on, she marked off the date every day. It was 8 May when there was a great deal of noise in the streets and the news spread all over the place: "The war has ended! The war has ended! The Germans have surrendered!"

We were very happy. "Can we go home now?" I asked my mother.

"I hope so," she said. "Let's go out to celebrate." It was the first time since my dad's death that I noticed Mum was in a good mood.

A large crowd had gathered down in the street. American jeeps were driving around with the soldiers singing and waving flags with red and white stripes and many white stars in a corner of blue. Mum told me that this was the American flag and each of the stars represented one state, forming the Union. There was singing and dancing in the streets and the soldiers shared drinks with the civilians. However, the locals who had remained to help run the place were remarkably quiet.

The celebration was soon replaced by uncertainty. My mother wanted to find out when we could go home. But no one knew. Then, there was an announcement that the Americans were leaving. I was very upset, since this was the end of my friendship with Henry. As the war had ended, there was no need for him to check for blackouts anymore.

One evening, he came to say goodbye. He shook my mum's hands and planted a kiss on the top of my head. We were very sad – he had become part of our life. I had always looked forward to his evening visits.

Since we'd been liberated from the camp, most people had been nice to us, knowing where we had come from, but it was only Henry who showed what my mum described as real kindness. He was interested in us, and we felt that if something bad happened, he would protect us.

At the end of May, the Americans left. But before they did, they announced that anybody who wanted to go with them could do so. They would settle us in the American Zone of Occupation. From there we could go to Palestine or apply for a visa to the United States of America. When asked, Mum explained where Palestine was. She said that many Jewish people wanted to go there, because this was the place where our ancestors had originally lived.

I did not want to go, but found the idea of travelling to America very exciting. When I told my mother, she didn't even want to listen.

"But Dad has died. And who is—?" I could not finish before Mum interrupted me. She was angry. Very angry.

"Who is what? Have you forgotten your brother? Your aunts and uncles? Zsuzsi? Our whole family?"

"I am sorry." I realized then that Mum wanted to go home more than anything. We were definitely not going to America.

The Americans told us that where we were, Hillersleben, and the area surrounding it would become the Soviet Zone of Occupation.

It was not the Russians, however, who arrived at the beginning of June, but the British. They spoke a language similar to the Americans, but it was slightly different. My mum explained that it was the same language; in fact, the Americans were speaking English but with a different accent.

We did not see much change in our lives, since the British continued running the place as the Americans had done. Only their uniforms were different and some of the soldiers wore skirts. I asked my mother about this.

"They're not skirts," she told me. "They're called kilts. Those soldiers are Scottish and this must be part of their uniform."

Unfortunately, the British did not stay long. According to Mum's diary, at the beginning of July the Russians arrived. And with their arrival life changed. And not for the better.

Soon after they arrived, the Russians running Hillersleben announced that a train would leave for Budapest on 2 July.

But it did not.

Mum was friendly with the couple next door, whose

daughter had died soon after liberation, and one day I saw her talking to the woman, Magda, in the kitchen. When their daughter, whose name I did not know, had died, my mother had fetched their food for them for a day or two afterwards. It was Magda who told Mum that the whole place would be cleared out by the end of July.

But it was not.

The supply and distribution of food had become less regular, and although we did not go hungry, there was less to eat. It was not unusual to see drunken Russian soldiers in the street. Although we did not go out after dark, my mother told me that we should be careful even during the day since the streets were not safe anymore.

As July turned into August and nothing happened, Mum became increasingly impatient. Although the Soviets promised imminent departures, there were no trains to Budapest. When the latest announced date of departure was postponed, she decided to take our fate into her own hands.

"We arrived here in mid-April," she said. "And now it's mid-August. That's four long months. In September you should go to school. If we don't do something, you will definitely miss your first year. The Russians keep promising, but they are doing nothing. We must do something."

And she did.

Chapter 9

Escape from the Russians

One morning Mum said that she was going with a small group of people to see the Russians. They were all eager to get home, and the previously promised date of departure had come to nothing.

"But you don't speak Russian," I objected. Even though I had witnessed how good her German was and even her attempt to talk to Henry in English, I was not so sure about this plan.

"No, I don't. But don't worry. We have a translator coming with us."

I asked whether I could go with her and she agreed. And so we went. It was the first time I had met Russian soldiers in their quarters, but I could immediately see the difference between Russian and American soldiers by their uniforms. In the summer, the American soldiers wore yellowish-brown shirts and matching trousers. Mum told me that the colour was "khaki", a word I had never heard.

The Russians' uniform was a pale greenish colour, and on the shoulder of the shirts there was a narrow board which, my mother explained, was to indicate the soldiers' rank. Most had leather belts with canvas bags hanging off them. It was not as nice as the American uniform, but much better than the black uniform of the SS guards. The Russian soldier we saw must have been an officer in charge since he had lots of medals on his chest.

At the end of the discussion Mum was disappointed and angry. All the commander had promised was yet another date.

So, she decided to act alone. We started visiting the railway station, and I soon realized that my mum was trying to get information about trains going east. Unfortunately, there were no trains to Hungary. The next big city, she explained, was Magdeburg.

She asked me not to tell anybody about our enquiries.

Despite these trips, it came as a surprise when one day my mother told me we were leaving that evening. She had hardly finished the sentence before she started to pack, taking only a few essential pieces, a couple of towels and bars of soap. In a separate bag she packed some food; I hadn't even noticed her preparing it.

And then we just walked out of Hillersleben.

Whether the Russians spotted us or not, we didn't know, but no one stopped us. I was rather excited, since we were starting yet another adventure. And this time we were going home. The fact that there were two of us and we were not in a crowd for once made it even more thrilling. But my enthusiasm disappeared when we arrived at the station and I couldn't see a passenger train. My mother pointed at an old, dirty goods train: "This is our—"

"We are not travelling on *that*?" I protested.

"Yes, we are. Or you could walk, of course."

"How far?"

"Not very far. Only a couple of hundred kilometres."

I looked at her and saw she was smiling. I realized there was no choice. We walked around the train, which already had an engine steaming, ready to go.

We climbed up the train on the side that couldn't be seen from the station. Mum helped me to get up and we settled in an open wagon. As we got in, we realized that the wagon was carrying coal.

I was disappointed but did not dare to say anything.

Mum was busy finding a space which was somewhat free of coal. She decided to stay in this wagon, because trying to find another one carrying less dirty cargo would have been too dangerous. We might have been discovered and taken back to Hillersleben.

There was a whistle and the train pulled slowly out of the station into the night. In an open wagon of coal, there wasn't much to do. However, I could look up at the sky. Fortunately, it was a clear night and the sky was full of stars. But I must have been exhausted, since I fell asleep.

When I woke up, it was morning – warm and sunny. Even the coal looked less dirty.

My mother produced breakfast: a slice of bread with salami and an apple. I asked for more, but she said that we didn't know when we would get more food. We still had to ration ourselves.

However, I enjoyed the journey in the sunshine. It was exciting. I had never felt this before: a combination of fun and danger. It was a new feeling – so different from the continuous fear in Bergen-Belsen. And although we were not really free, no one could tell us what to do and where to go and when. It was Mum who was in charge.

And it was such a relief after the camp. Life there was

boring: one day was just like the next, the only difference being that the next day was always worse than the previous. Getting into the open wagon, only the two of us, promised new adventures.

In the end there was no danger. No one found us to ask questions. We didn't even know when we crossed the border, but it must have been when the train stopped for a long time. Although I wanted to move, Mum said we should not. We might be discovered. As the train restarted, she said that we had left Germany.

"It's such a relief," she said. "We are now in Czechoslovakia."

"How do you know?"

"I could see signs on the road and at the station where we stopped. They were not in German – so must have been in Czech."

Soon we arrived at a very large station.

"We're in Prague," Mum told me.

"Where is Prague?"

"It's the capital of Czechoslovakia. It's east from where we were in Germany. We're now nearer, but still very far from Budapest."

"How far?"

"I don't know, but it must be hundreds and hundreds of kilometres."

"How are we going to get there?"

"By getting another train."

Our goods train stopped outside the station. We climbed down from our wagon: dirty and stiff. I could hardly move my legs and arms, and neither could Mum. But she was not to be defeated.

"We need to find a washroom or a toilet where we can clean up," she said, and we were on our way into the station. I had never seen such a large building or so many people. They all seemed to be in hurry. Not looking left or right, they moved through the crowd, sometimes pushing people out of their way. Mum would not let my hand out of her grip.

"Why are there so many people here? And where are they going?" I asked.

"I don't know where they're going. All over Europe, I suppose. Since the war has ended, the whole world seems to be travelling: soldiers, ex-prisoners like us from concentration camps, people who have lost their homes and families. Prague is at a crossroads between east and west."

Finally, we got to a quieter part of the station and found a large toilet. There was a big sign with two letters, "WC", and something beneath it in much smaller writing. There was another sign with the same big letters but what was written beneath was different. My mother looked at both and then decided: "You come with me to the women's."

"But I want to go to the other one, with the men."

"No."

From the way she said it, I knew that I should not argue. Reluctantly I went with her.

Mum produced a towel and a bar of soap and we washed ourselves as best as we could. We looked and felt better.

"Now, we need to find a train to Budapest," Mum said.

In the meantime, next to one of the tracks, not very far away, I spotted a stall with an odd flag above it. I hadn't seen a flag like it before. It had a red cross in the middle of a white background.

"What flag is it?" I asked.

"Where do you see a flag?"

When I pointed in the direction of the stall, Mum said, "Oh, that one? It's the flag of the Red Cross."

"What is a red cross?"

"It isn't *a* red cross. It's *the* Red Cross. Don't you remember the rare feasts when we had better food in the camp? It all came from the Red Cross. I explained it to you then. It's an international organization which helps people in need – during and after wars."

"Will they help Jews?"

"Why do you ask?"

"Because they have the cross and we are Jewish."

"Of course they will, silly boy."

"So they would help us?"

And before she could answer, I was off. When I got to the stall a few people were waiting. My mum followed me. One of the women was giving out slices of bread, while the other distributed small bottles of milk. When it was my turn, I got the bread and milk. I said in English, "Thank you," while Mum thanked them in German.

As we left the stall, I stopped and asked, "Can I get another portion?"

"I don't think you can."

"I'm still hungry."

She explained that everybody could have only one portion, since we mustn't eat other hungry people's food.

"If you go back, they will recognize you and you won't get any."

Suddenly I had an idea: "Can I have my jumper?

"What for? It's very warm."

"You'll see," I said and, putting on the jumper, I went back to the stall. It was a good time to go, as there was nobody in front of me. The two women looked at me and then at each other, but after a short hesitation, I received my second helping.

As I joined Mum, who looked at me disapprovingly, she said, "You shouldn't have done that. Do you think that they didn't recognize you, despite your disguise?"

One of the women was waving at us. It was obvious, as I had already suspected, that my little ploy had backfired: they had clearly recognized me. Now they were going to reclaim the bread and milk. To prevent this, I quickly drank the milk, but could not quite finish eating the bread before we arrived at the stall.

The woman who had waved to us said something in German and Mum answered in the same language. Instead of an angry scene, both smiled. As we left, I asked, "What did she say?"

"She said that I have a terrible son and should change him for a better one."

"I don't believe you."

"She said that I have a very enterprising son."

The only thing now was to find a train home. It took a long time to find one that travelled directly to Budapest without changes. The train was crowded, but we managed to find seats in a compartment. At first I didn't know how we had paid for the tickets, but then remembered that we had got some money from the Americans. Mum had told me at the time that it came from an American Jewish organization.

Although we did not know what might happen from one day to the next, everything had changed for the better. And this train was taking us home. I was dreaming of being reunited with my toys and seeing my brother Gyuri again. Even my mother seemed to smile more often.

We could not know the surprises that were in store for us.

Chapter 10

Shock in Budapest

Although the seats were very hard, we were lucky to be able to sit. People were standing in the corridors and some were even sitting outside on the steps, until the ticket collector ordered them inside. We had several long, unexpected stops in the middle of nowhere and Mum was concerned that we may not even get to Budapest. But eventually, we did.

I didn't know when we crossed the border, but my mum said that we were back in Hungary.

Finally home.

Mum told me that, it being the end of August, we had been away for well over a year – more than fourteen months, in fact. More still if we added the time in the ghetto. It was a long time, and it seemed much longer.

I could tell that she was nervous when she said, "I don't know what we're going to find at home. We've already lost your dad and grandma. I do hope that all the others survived."

I did not know who she was thinking of, but I was certain that my brother Gyuri was at the top of her list. While we were away, she had frequently talked about him: how bright and how kind he was to everybody. Sometimes I was jealous. I thought that I would never be able to live up to his reputation.

In Hillersleben she had even prepared a homecoming present for him. One day, she opened a tin containing what looked like thick cream and poured it into a saucepan with cubes of butter, which was not easy to get, and some brown sugar. When heated, it smelled mouth-watering.

"What are you cooking?" I'd asked.

"I'm making fudge."

"For us?" I was eager to have some.

"No, it's a present for Gyuri."

"But Gyuri isn't here."

"It's a homecoming present for him. We'll give it to him when we arrive in Makó."

"So we can't eat it?"

"No, you can't. Anyway, you had your chocolate from your American friend."

"Oh, that's different."

"All right, when it's ready you can taste it."

When it was ready, Mum cut it up into cubes and gave me a piece to taste. It was delicious! I could have eaten the whole lot. Instead, I licked up the crumbs from the tray.

She found a small box – it must have been for a child's shoes – in the wardrobe and put the pieces of fudge inside, one by one. The remaining space she filled with crunched up newspapers. When I asked why she was doing this, she explained that it would prevent pieces of fudge being thrown about in the half-filled box and getting broken up. I understood that the fudge was very precious.

As we eventually left the train in Budapest we were immediately surrounded by a sea of people. The station was even busier than the one in Prague. I noticed there were many Russian soldiers in uniform and farmers from the country. The women were carrying large wicker baskets full of fruit and vegetables for the market. We could hardly wait to leave.

The station was at the end of a large square, which was made even larger by missing houses. They had been bombed and some of the ruins had not been cleared. After we surveyed the sight with disbelief, we walked down the steps of the station. Mum knew exactly where we wanted to go: to Aunt Márta and Uncle Lajos's flat.

Aunt Márta was one of Dad's four sisters and Mum's favourite. Márta and Lajos didn't have children and their love was directed at Gyuri and me. They didn't live far from the station. A wide avenue led from the square towards the Danube, and their flat was down a side street. It was in a Jewish district which had become part of the ghetto. Their block was a modern building and they lived on the top floor.

The lift did not work so we climbed up to the fourth floor. Mum pressed the bell and, after a minute or two, we heard shuffling inside and a key being inserted into the lock and turned.

Aunt Márta appeared in a narrow opening. When she saw us, she cried out: "Ili! Peter!" She flung the door wide open, but not as wide as her arms to embrace us. Behind her, Uncle Lajos waited with a warm but calmer greeting.

Aunt Márta was a small, round woman with pale skin like Dad's. She and my mother always got on well and were fond of each other.

Uncle Lajos was even smaller, and when he sat in an armchair his feet did not reach the ground but dangled above the carpet. In contrast to Aunt Márta, his skin was quite brown. I knew them better than other members of my dad's family.

We were still standing in the hall with the open door

behind us, when Aunt Márta seemed to panic, suddenly realizing that somebody was missing. The picture she was looking at was not complete. "Where is—?"

Mum did not allow her to finish. "He died. In Bergen-Belsen. On 13 March."

We were still standing in the hall. I was very tired and wanted to sit down, but Aunt Márta just stood there, like a statue, tears streaming down her face.

It was Mum who now embraced her.

Uncle Lajos turned around and opened the door of their living room. "Don't stand in the hall," he said. We entered their large, sunlit room.

"Do sit down," Uncle Lajos said. "You must be tired."

"Yes, we are," I said.

Mum and Aunt Márta sat on the sofa, Uncle Lajos and I in armchairs.

Aunt Márta could not wait any longer. "What happened?"

Mum described Dad's death and how he exchanged his bread ration for cigarettes. She didn't mention that even the extra slice, which she had earned for him by washing other people's dirty linen, also went up in smoke.

"You see –" my aunt turned to my uncle – "you should give up smoking. You're ruining your health."

Uncle Lajos was a passionate smoker, and it was rare to see

him without a cigarette dangling from his mouth or between his fingers or resting in an ashtray waiting to be lifted. The index and middle fingers of his right hand, just like Dad's, were stained brown from the cigarettes. Although Aunt Márta had strong views, she was losing this war against smoking.

"Do you know where he has been buried?"

"No, I don't," answered Mum. "I don't even know *whether* he was buried. You can't imagine what the camps were like towards the end. It's beyond imagination. People aren't going to believe…"

I thought Mum would cry, but she didn't.

It was Aunt Márta who did. Then, after a moment, she stood up and asked, "What can I get for you? Do you want to eat?"

"A little bit later," Mum answered. "Do you have coffee? And a glass of milk for Peter."

Aunt Márta disappeared into the kitchen and Uncle Lajos uttered his first words since he had learned the details of my dad's death: "I'm so sorry. Márta loved your husband and so did I. She has lost so many…"

At that moment my aunt came back into the room carrying a tray with coffee, a milk jug, a sugar bowl and a glass of milk. I immediately noticed a couple of biscuits on a small plate.

"This is for you," said Aunt Márta, and handed the small plate with the biscuits and the glass of milk to me.

"Lajos started to talk about your family losses…" Mum said.

"He should have waited," Aunt Márta replied. "But perhaps it's better to get it over with."

As she started talking, I found it difficult to swallow the biscuits and stopped munching.

My aunt and uncle had been lucky: they were not deported but their flat had become part of the Budapest ghetto. The battle for the city had been terrible, my uncle said. It lasted for months. The retreating Germans blew up all the beautiful bridges over the Danube. The Hungarian fascists – members of an extreme right-wing party who had terrorized the population – had not had time to deport the Jews but rounded many up and lined them along the quay of the river, where they machine-gunned them. The river had become red with blood.

"What happened to your other sisters and brothers?" asked my mother. "They all lived in the country."

There was a silence before my aunt started to speak again. All three of her sisters, along with their husbands, had been deported and murdered in Auschwitz. I had never heard of Auschwitz before, or if I had I didn't remember. But soon I learned never to forget it. Fortunately, they hadn't had children. One of Aunt Márta's brothers, Pista, had died with his wife and younger son, but the elder son, Gabi, disappeared from the concentration camp.

"Disappeared?" Mum interrupted.

"Without trace. We couldn't find his name in the central register of disappeared persons."

Aunt Márta's youngest brother, Misi, survived with his wife, as did Bandi, the eldest of the four brothers, but his wife and daughter had died.

I saw that on hearing each name my mum became more and more frozen. She said nothing. But she did not cry. As for me, I only vaguely remembered these relations: we had rarely met them even before the war. I knew the names but could not put faces to them.

There was silence again. My aunt looked at my uncle, who nodded. Then Aunt Márta spoke: "I didn't know whether to tell you or not, but perhaps it's better if you hear it from me."

My mother put down the coffee cup and suddenly stood up.

"Gyuri has died. He died a couple of weeks ago on the sixth of August."

The silence was broken by my mother's cry – a cry I had

never heard before. It was more like the howl of a wounded animal. As if all the suffering of the previous months had found an expression in this terrible news.

My aunt and uncle stood up and walked towards my mum, Aunt Márta embracing her. I just stood there, not quite understanding what had happened. I wanted to cry, but couldn't.

Aunt Márta, still holding Mum in her arms, gently led her to the sofa, sat her down and took the space next to her. Mum's crying turned into sobs. She asked, "What happened?"

"I don't know all the details; your brother Jenő, who is in Makó, will tell you more. Gyuri came back from hard labour. Despite having lost weight, he was well. His great news was that he had been admitted to university. He was happy and waiting for you. Then he became ill; he was admitted to the local hospital and died. When Jenő told me, I couldn't believe it."

I walked over to Mum, she extended her arm and pulled me towards her.

Suddenly I remembered the fudge she had made for Gyuri.

"Mum, can I have the fudge?"

Mum looked at me with a vacant stare, which terrified

me. It was like the one she had in Bergen-Belsen when she was admitted to the hospital.

"Yes," she said. She handed me the box and turned away.

I took it, but I was unable to open it.

It was then that I started to cry.

Chapter 11

Homecoming

It took some time for my mum to feel strong enough to make the journey home. She wanted to continue to Makó straight away, but on this occasion Aunt Márta put her foot down and convinced her to stay for at least one more night. In the afternoon, my uncle suggested that we should have a walk. We slowly made our way down the main boulevard towards the Danube.

I could not believe what I saw.

There were ruins everywhere: not only houses but whole blocks and long runs of streets had disappeared. The most dramatic picture of all waited for us when we arrived at the quay of the Danube. Just as my uncle had said, the bridges spanning the river had all been blown up.

Uncle Lajos said that the battle between the German

Army, supported by their Hungarian allies, and the Red Army had lasted well over three months.

The next day, we took the train to Makó. We were going to leave from a different station this time. However, we learned that the train did not go directly to my hometown, but only to Szeged. The railway bridge over the Tisza had also been blown up. There was a bus service, which would take us from Szeged station to the other side of the river.

As we got on to the crowded train, my mum asked, "Do you know how many train journeys we've made?"

"No, I don't, but it's easy to count. Makó to Szeged: one. Szeged to Strasshof: two. Strasshof to Bergen-Belsen: three. Bergen-Belsen to Farsleben: four. Hillersleben to Magdeburg: five. Magdeburg to Prague: six. Prague to Budapest: seven. And Budapest to Makó: eight. We've done eight train journeys. And two bus journeys, of course – from Farsleben to Hillersleben and the ride just now across the Tisza."

"Well done, Peter. We made eight train journeys."

"I must have travelled more than most children."

"And how many countries have we been in?"

"Austria, Germany and what was the last? Yes ... Czechoslovakia. Three, if we don't count Hungary."

"Correct. But we're coming to the end of our journey. We're going to arrive soon."

The last few kilometres after months and months of travelling seemed never-ending. The carriage was full and the heat was remorseless. The wind blew soot through the open window, which soon covered everything and got into my left eye. When I blinked, it felt scratchy. Mum got out her handkerchief and asked me to look up and then down. Somehow, she managed to remove the irritating tiny piece from my eye.

As the train was crossing the railway bridge over the Maros – fortunately, this one had not been destroyed – the engine sounded its whistle and a few minutes later the train pulled into the station.

No one was waiting for us, but we had not expected anybody.

We started to walk.

The house where we had lived before deportation was not very far from the station, but instead of walking towards it, Mum took a different direction along a wide, tree-lined street which led towards the centre of town.

"Aren't we going home?" I asked.

"Home? Why should we go there? There's nobody living there anymore. We're going to your grandparents' house."

I was not sure what Mum meant. After all, I had been born there and we had lived there until we had to go to the ghetto. Suddenly, I understood. Dad had died in Bergen-Belsen; Gyuri had died in the hospital. No one was waiting for us.

I felt I shouldn't ask any questions, and for now we continued our walk and soon reached a narrow side street which led to the timber yard.

"Let's have a look." It was the first time since we had learned of Gyuri's death that my mother had showed any interest in the outside world. Soon we reached the main gate. The place was deserted. The two villas flanking the timber yard were equally without any life. If we had walked through the yard, we would have reached our house from the back, but we did not. Anyway, the place was locked: we wouldn't have been able to get in.

We turned back and continued our walk to my grandparents' home, the family home. We never went back to live in our old house again.

When we arrived at my grandparents' house, my mum hesitated before we entered, as if to strengthen herself for what we might find. At last, we went in through the garden at the side of the house. We walked up the stairs leading into the hall. Surprisingly, we found an unmade bed, two chairs and a small bedside table in the garden room. It was called this because it was the only room which faced the large garden at the back. We then walked through the rest of the house and discovered that all the other rooms were empty.

The beautiful wooden floor, specially made from the timber yard's best material, was naked: all the lovely carpets with their striking colours and geometrical patterns had disappeared. Even the pictures on the walls had all gone. Only the oil portraits of my grandparents looked down at us from the wall of the dining room.

"Is anybody at home?" Mum shouted.

We heard footsteps, the door opened and Uncle Jenő entered. He embraced and kissed my mum. "Ili, I thought you would never return." Then he bowed down to plant a kiss on the top of my head. "How you've grown," he told me.

As I looked up at him, I saw that he, unlike me, had become smaller, having developed a stoop. But he looked well apart from this.

"Uncle, you look very suntanned," I told him.

"Oh, yes. I've been going to swim in the river. We're having a good summer."

His words brought back the memory of that distant

summer when Dad had taught me to swim and I'd jealously watched Gyuri leaving us behind.

Mum looked around the empty room at the naked walls and floor.

"Where has all our furniture gone?"

"I don't know. I tried to recover some of it, but without much success."

"That I can see. When we were deported, didn't the officials make a list of the things we had left behind?"

Even I remembered when the town officials had come around with the gendarmes.

"Well, at least they couldn't steal the portraits of our parents."

"Why not?" I interrupted.

"Because everybody in town would know whose property they were from," said my mum. "We should try again to recover at least a couple of pieces. Look, we are quite tired, can we sit down?"

"Yes, of course."

We walked into the garden room and Uncle Jenő hastily made up his bed.

"I use this room and the bathroom next door. You two should sit in the chair," he said, while he flopped down on to the bed.

There was silence. I knew what was going to happen next.

"What happened to Gyuri?" Mum asked.

"Didn't Márta tell you?" replied Uncle Jenő.

"She did. But I want to it hear from you."

"He was admitted to hospital on the eighteenth of July with a high temperature and stomach pains. He died on the sixth of August at 3 p.m."

"Do you know the cause of death?"

"Yes. 'Abdominal fever' was on the death certificate."

"So, it must have been typhoid fever."

"Yes. It was a tragedy. I had it too, but recovered. "

"You were in hospital too?"

"Yes, but only for a couple of days."

"And Gyuri visited you?"

"Yes."

There was a long silence. I didn't know what my mum was going to do next. For a while she did not look at her brother, then she asked, "You know that Mother died?"

Uncle Jenő nodded.

"In Strasshof. Before we got to Bergen-Belsen. Did you know that we were in Bergen-Belsen?"

"Yes." Uncle Jenő nodded again. "Someone who came home earlier told me she had seen you there. She also knew that Sándor had died." It was strange to hear Dad's name, as it always was, since Mum referred to him as "your dad".

"Yes. Do you know what happened to the others?" Mum asked.

"Yes, I do."

"Szerén?" She was the eldest of the three sisters.

My uncle told us that she had survived with her husband, Menyhért, and their daughter, Magda, and granddaughter, Erika. They weren't deported because they lived in Romania and the Romanians didn't deport them.

"Margit?" She was the middle of the three sisters.

Uncle continued to say that my aunt Margit, her husband, Mihály, and their teenage son, Pista, all ended up in Auschwitz. "They were gassed. They lived in the wrong part of Transylvania."

"Manó?" He was the eldest of the five brothers.

"He survived with Anci and Vera and András." Anci was my aunt, and Vera and András my cousins. Uncle Jenő paused as if to collect strength. "But our other three brothers all died. Their deaths have now been confirmed."

My mother had told me that before the deportation these uncles were all taken to the eastern front for hard labour. Since there was no news from them for a long time, we thought they must have frozen to death.

Mum was sitting motionless and said nothing. She didn't cry. By now she must have been running out of tears.

Then I plucked up the courage and asked what I had wanted to ask some time ago.

"What happened to Aunt Anna and Zsuzsi?"

My uncle looked at me.

"They were murdered in Auschwitz."

Auschwitz, I thought, *that name again.*

In the long silence, I started to count the dead in the family. I stopped at twenty-one. Suddenly I started to cry and only stopped when my mother hugged me.

In the end, Mum's first visit was not to the furniture depot to try to get back some of our furniture, but to the Jewish cemetery. After some difficulty, she found a taxi driver who would agree to take us.

The Jewish cemetery was outside town, in the middle of some fields. No paved road led there. In the autumn and winter, when too much rain or snow fell, it was impossible to get there, and taxi drivers were reluctant to undertake the journey.

Now, though, it was a sunny end-of-summer day, and we easily reached the cemetery. Mum asked the driver to wait for us.

Although Uncle Jenő had described where Gyuri's grave was, it was not easy to find. The whole place was neglected. The caretaker had probably not been paid while we were away, and he had not done anything. Many of the graves were overgrown with weeds, which were everywhere.

Finally, we found Gyuri's plot. It was a makeshift grave with a small stone on which his name and the dates of his birth and death were painted. Mum prayed and I prayed with her. She cried and I cried with her.

Then we went to find my grandfather's grave. It was not difficult to locate, since it was very large with a beautiful white marble tombstone. I saw that he had died long ago, in 1933.

A week later, my mum decided to erect another beautiful marble tombstone for Gyuri. On the same tombstone, my dad was also remembered. Although Gyuri's body was in the grave, we did not know where my dad's was.

It was Mum's idea, approved by her surviving sister and two brothers, that all the other members of the family who were killed during the war should have their names engraved on my grandfather's large stone. The tombstone had been designed to accommodate Grandma when she died, and her name was included, according to her wish.

However, there were now a further eight names. And

since the places where they died were unknown, an additional sentence was added: "They died somewhere in Europe."

All those who had been deported and died during the war were commemorated every year at a special service in the synagogue on the anniversary of our deportation on 16 June. As part of the service, all the names were monotonously read out from a long list by the cantor. His strong voice trembled when he read out the names of his own wife and young daughter. Later, I took pride in the fact that more names were read from my family than from any other.

The first night, we decided to sleep on the floor and Uncle Jenő managed to find some bed linen. We didn't need much, as it was still warm, but the floor was very hard. It was a strange first night to be at home. Unfortunately, we couldn't say that, after all that time, we were finally sleeping in our own beds!

My mother didn't waste any time starting a new life. She and Uncle Jenő went to a depot to recover some more furniture and managed to claim back some pieces. Within a day or two, she had restarted the kitchen. With fresh food from the market, Mum cooked simple but mouth-watering meals. She cleaned the bathroom and made sure that everything was working.

After a week or so we had our first visitors. Aunt Márta and Uncle Lajos came. They wanted to see us, but their visit also served another purpose: they needed to get food from the market. I had to give up my new bed temporarily, but since I loved them, I did not grumble.

Aunt Márta also gave me a present: a round gold disk on a thin gold chain. On the disk there was an engraving with the words: *From Márta to Peter*. This, she explained, I should wear around my neck.

It was autumn when something unexpected happened which changed our life. Our large house with only three people living in it, and its central position in a beautiful street, attracted the attention of the occupying Russian forces. It was also a couple of hundred metres from the police headquarters.

I did not understand why the Russians were staying in town. My mother explained: "You remember that Hungary was an ally of Germany in the war. But when our country wanted peace with the Americans and British, the Germans invaded us. This is the reason why we were deported. You understand?" I nodded. "The Russians defeated the

Germans and liberated Hungary. Now they are staying as an occupying force. You understand?" I nodded again, although it seemed very complicated.

"How long are they staying?"

"I don't know. No one does. As long as they want: they are the victors."

One day, a couple of Russian soldiers and an officer appeared. They surveyed the house then went away. However, the next day the officer came back and stayed. We were told that he was going to be billeted with us and would stay until the garrison left town.

We learned that his name was Sacha. He was tall and slim with straw-coloured hair and blue eyes. During the following months, we got accustomed to his presence in the house and even got to like him. In a strange way, he became part of our everyday life. Uncle Jenő started to learn Russian and his knowledge was of great help later on.

Even before Sacha moved in, a truckload of furniture arrived for him and was unloaded into the largest corner room of the house. There were too many pieces to fit in his room and those he did not want found their way into our near-empty rooms. It was funny to look at the hotchpotch of things: so different from what had been there before.

Sacha had many visitors. His guests were usually soldiers,

and occasionally he invited Uncle Jenő, who was happy to join in. They sang in Russian: their songs were either very jolly and fast or sad and slow.

They also seemed to drink a lot, since there were usually many empty bottles after the parties. They were different from wine bottles, and when I asked Uncle Jenő what they were he told me that they contained vodka.

"It's a spirit," my uncle explained. "Very strong. Do you know what *pálinka* is?" I nodded. "It's like *pálinka*, but without the taste of apricot or plum."

"So, if it doesn't have a taste, why do you drink it?"

"When you grow up, you'll learn."

However, not all Sacha's visitors were men. Some were women; they were loud and wore dresses with lots of colours – dresses my mother and my aunts would never wear. Their lips were painted blood-red. On the occasions when they were in the house, Mum made sure that I was out of the way and often sent me into the garden.

One day, something very upsetting happened. Mum and I were alone in the house when a Russian soldier arrived and asked for Sacha. When my mum explained with a mixture of sign language and a couple of the Russian words we had all picked up that Sacha was not at home, the soldier left.

Later, as I was coming back in from the garden, I heard

shouts from the dining room and recognized my mother's – very upset – voice, along with a loud Russian one. Mum repeatedly shouted in Russian, "*Niet, niet,*" which I knew meant "no". I opened the door of the dining room and was terrified by what I saw.

The Russian soldier had returned and was apparently chasing my mother around the dining table. Zsuzsi and I used to do this for fun, but my mum was clearly frightened. When I entered, they froze, standing at opposite ends of the table. There were a couple of overturned chairs between them.

Seeing me, the soldier did not move for a moment, but then resumed the chase. Mum pushed the only chair that remained standing in front of him. He could not stop and fell over it, but he got up again and carried on trying to catch her.

I decided to step between them to prevent him reaching her. He was panting and I could smell alcohol on his breath. At that moment, the door opened and Sacha entered. We all froze.

Then everything happened in quick succession.

Sacha surveyed the scene and, without saying a single word, took a couple of steps towards the soldier. He drew a gun and, with its butt, hit him. I heard the crack of a bone and a spray of blood spread over the white tablecloth. Sacha talked to my mum – sentences I didn't understand, but which must have been an apology.

When Uncle Jenő returned in the evening, he went to have a drink with Sacha. Sacha further apologized to my uncle, who later translated for us. After this, Uncle Jenő still drank with the Russians, helped by his increasing knowledge of their language, but this incident somehow changed our relationship with them. In the end we were happy when they left. Sacha's large room became ours again.

In the spring of 1946, I developed a terrible pain in my throat. I could hardly swallow and could only drink fluids. My mother immediately took me to a doctor with a long name who was an ear, nose and throat specialist. She was also concerned that I might be losing weight again.

Since we'd been home, Mum had cooked good, tasty food to make sure that I ate well and put on some weight. Part of this diet was a large cup of hot chocolate that I had to drink every evening before bed. I'd liked this at the beginning, but after a few months it had become boring.

The ear-nose-throat man didn't mention my weight, but he diagnosed tonsillitis. He explained that there was a pair of glands at the back of my throat and these were inflamed.

They had become larger as well as painful. They had to be removed, he said. The idea frightened me.

"Why?"

"If we don't remove them, the glands become even larger and more painful. You won't be able to swallow."

I looked at Mum, hoping for help, but she nodded.

"Are you going to do it now?"

"No. It has to be done in hospital."

"I don't want to go to hospital."

My mother intervened. "Don't argue. You have to," she said.

"When?"

"Tomorrow," said Ear-nose-throat. "The sooner the better."

"Will it be painful?"

"No. You won't even notice it. You'll be asleep."

The next day I was admitted to hospital and they operated the following morning. The specialist and a nurse were waiting for me, all in white. I was tied down and a large disc was forced over my face. I wanted to get up and run away, but I couldn't. There was a terrible smell and I was gasping for air but couldn't breathe.

Then everything went black.

When I woke up, I saw my mum's smiling face. I wanted to speak but couldn't. Then the specialist came to look at me.

"Open your mouth," he said. He must have been pleased by what he saw. "He'll be all right. The operation was very straightforward, but the tonsils had to come out."

Later Uncle Jenő arrived with Sacha and they brought a large tub of ice cream. Since I couldn't eat anything solid, I enjoyed the ice cream more than ever before. After a couple of days, I could go home.

On the way home, I asked my mum how much the operation had cost. At first, I didn't understand what she was saying. It hadn't cost any money, but the agreed price was a certain amount of grain. "Money is now worth nothing," Mum said, "since there has been such terrible inflation."

"What's inflation?"

"When money loses its value."

"How can it lose its value? It tells you on the coins and on the banknotes what it's worth, doesn't it?"

"Those numbers you see don't mean anything now. The coins have gone out of circulation; they are completely worthless. The notes are continuously reprinted with an increasing number of zeros at the end. I was asked to pay in grain, since money has no value."

I still was not quite sure what it all meant. Not until we went to the cinema. Going to the movies was the only entertainment in town. One of the two cinemas was less than a couple of minutes' walk away from our house.

As we got to the box office, my mother produced four eggs from a small paper bag. She handed them to a cashier, who in turn gave us the tickets. Suddenly it all became clear: we paid with eggs for the entry and not with money.

Fortunately, this madness did not last long. That same summer, the banknotes with the many zeros disappeared and crisp new money was introduced. The name of the new currency was the *forint* which replaced the *pengő*.

And with the new money, the family's fortunes turned for the better.

Soon after we returned, Mum suggested to Uncle Jenő that they should restart the family business, the timber yard. Uncle Jenő agreed, but he had doubts: "Ili, you don't have any experience and nor have I. Do you think—?"

Mum interrupted him: "We're going to get it, don't you worry. However, first we should get permission from the other owners. They'll agree, since there is no reason why they shouldn't."

"And where are we going to get money to start with?" Uncle Jenő asked.

"We're going to borrow it. But wait a minute ... we might have some money... Do we have a spade?"

"Are you going to start gardening?"

"I'd nearly forgotten. There's some in the garden."

"They say money doesn't grow on trees, and it certainly doesn't grow in the ground."

"You wouldn't have known, because you'd already been taken for hard labour, but we hid some cash and a couple of pieces of jewellery in the ground. Mother asked me to do it for her. Come on, let's see whether we can find it," Mum said.

We went out into the garden, and on the way Uncle Jenő picked up a spade from the garden shed. We stopped where the fruit trees were. Mum looked around: "This is it," she said, pointing at an apricot tree. She started to dig around the trunk of the tree and after a while the spade hit something. She dug a little bit more, bent over and lifted out a large glass jar. She wiped the earth from the glass and forced the lid open.

My mother's smile disappeared when she pulled out a handful of pulp.

"Oh, the water must have seeped in. We thought it was waterproof." She sighed and started digging again.

"Now what are you looking for?" my uncle asked.

"There was another jar with the jewellery in it," my mum

explained. "If only it's survived."

"Even if we could have sold some jewellery, it wouldn't be enough," said Uncle Jenő, disappointed. "Stop, Ili." He took the spade from Mum, seeing that her shoulders sagged.

"We might have had some other jewellery," my mum said regretfully. "Before we were deported, I was going to leave a couple of pieces with one of our neighbours for safekeeping. Mrs Szabó was always friendly and I thought she just might help, but Sándor was worried we'd get her in trouble."

In the end, my mother and Uncle Jenő had to borrow money to restart the family business with the permission of the two other surviving family members – Uncle Manó, who lived with his family in Makó, and Aunt Szerén, who by that time was in Palestine. Mum thought that Uncle Manó, who had previous business experience, should be the director, but he declined. At the time, he was already running his own independent business exporting grain.

This is how Mum and Uncle Jenő started to run the timber yard. My mother was right. They did learn what to do, and soon the timber yard changed beyond recognition: it came fully back to life.

Soon they were employing around a hundred workers,

Uncle Jenő told me.

I could see it for myself because I was still not at school, having missed a year, and Mum occasionally took me with her. It was great fun to roam around the place, but I missed Zsuzsi terribly. When I crossed the yard, I always thought of her: somehow this place belonged to both of us. However, I still enjoyed visiting, and some of the workers must have liked me, since they let me sit on the cart with them.

The success of the business reflected in our daily life. Soon, Mum was employing a full-time maid, who lived with us in the house. Apart from cleaning, she often cooked when Mum was at the timber yard. From early spring to late autumn a young man came once a week to look after the garden. After long neglect, it looked better than ever.

As the summer of 1946 came to an end, I knew my life was going to change, once again.

At the start of September, I was going to school.

Chapter 12

My first day at school

It is very difficult to describe how excited I was. It was a mixture of expectation and fear. While I was very eager to start, I also had many worries and doubts. One was that I had missed a year. When we arrived home, the schools were just starting, but even if we had arrived earlier, I was not ready to go. According to my mum, I was too weak and still too thin after months of starvation.

I had also had experiences that other children my age had not. This must have made me different, I thought, made me stand out. And there was another reason which frightened me more than any other: I was going to a Catholic school.

I had overheard a conversation between Mum and Uncle Jenő earlier in the summer. It was the raised voice of Uncle Jenő that had made me listen:

"Why on earth would you send the poor boy to a Catholic school?"

"For two reasons. First, it's the best school in town, and second, it's the nearest. Before I get him admitted, I'll make all the necessary enquiries."

And she did. Well before my first day at school, my mother asked me to sit down and said she wanted to talk to me. I knew immediately that it was something important. Something important was always introduced by "I want to talk to you." And this was really important.

She told me that I was going to a Catholic school and repeated what I already knew: it was the best in town and the nearest. I knew at the very beginning that any protest was in vain. She had talked to the head teacher and my future form teacher. They were very happy to have me. They knew our family, she said. They also knew what had happened to us in the war.

"Will there be any other Jewish children?" I asked.

"I don't know for sure, but it's unlikely."

"So, I will be the only Jewish boy?"

"Quite possibly. They aren't going to eat you."

"But they teach a different religion."

"Yes, they do. But you can leave the class during religious education: you have an exemption."

"But what about—?"

"You want to learn about your own religion. Don't worry, I've already fixed it up. You'll go to a special class in Judaism at the Jewish community centre."

So, it was all arranged.

Nevertheless, I couldn't sleep the night before going to school on that first day.

The next morning, my mum gave me a pair of nice shorts, a white shirt and a light jumper to put on. She came with me to the school, which really was very near to our house. Mum stopped at the gate, kissed me and said, "Don't worry. Everything will be all right. I'm not going to work today; I've told your uncle. I'll be waiting for you here at the end of lessons."

I walked through the gate and started to walk towards the school. After a few steps I stopped. I wanted to turn back and go home with Mum. I turned around, but Mum had gone. I was frightened. Frightened of the school, of all the teachers and of all the children I didn't know.

Suddenly I thought of Gyuri, then Dad, then Grandma, then Zsuzsi, then Aunt Anna and all the others. And, as if by magic, I was seeing them.

I started to walk towards the school, at first hesitantly and then with more confidence. *I will be like Gyuri*, I thought. *I will do my best. I will be at the top of my class.*

Someone shouted my name from the door of the school: "Hurry up, you'll be late!"

I ran the last few metres.

I did not know it then, but it was at this moment that my life, which had hovered between survival and death, became firmly anchored in hope.

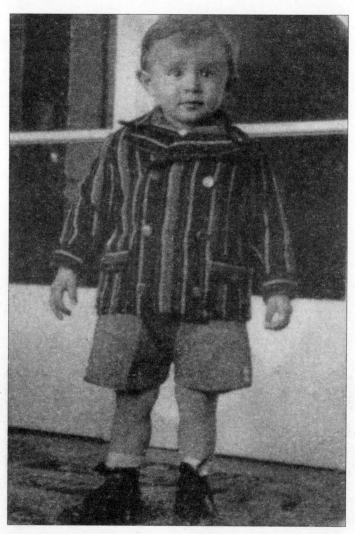

Me, aged around three.

You may want to know...

What happened next

Peter, me

I did enjoy going to the Catholic school, but my time there
did not last long: after two years everything changed. The
Communists came into power in Hungary, and in 1949 they
banned the teaching of religion in schools.

I finished elementary school at the end of June 1954 and
went on to the same high school that Gyuri had attended.
In October 1956, when I was seventeen, our regular life was
abruptly and dramatically interrupted yet again.

Following anti-government demonstrations and riots, a
revolution swept away the Communist order and Hungary
became a free country for ten days. On 4 November, the
Russian Red Army entered Budapest and a desperate and
uneven battle began, which lasted a few weeks.

Me, aged around nine.

There was no fighting in Makó, only demonstrations in favour of freedom for the country, in which I took part. With Soviet help, the restoration of dictatorship did not take very long. The revenge and ensuing oppression, however, lasted for years.

Me, aged around ten.

At the age of seventeen, I had decided to become a doctor. My experiences during the war might have been one of the determining factors. I wanted to have a profession in which I could help people in need.

Despite my good results, my admission to the Medical University of Szeged was fraught with difficulties, as a result of coming from a family that was wealthier and more successful than average. The Communist government did not like anyone who showed enterprise.

In the end, though, I qualified in 1964. Two years later I was fortunate to receive an offer to do medical research in London.

I got on a plane in the afternoon of 31 October 1968 at Budapest airport and arrived a couple of hours later in London. As a young doctor I received a fellowship from the Wellcome Trust, a large medical charity that promotes research, to work in London for a year. However, at the end of the year, I refused to return home. For this, as both a punishment and a warning to others not to follow my example, I was put on trial by the Communist government in Hungary. I was sentenced – fortunately in my absence – to sixteen months in prison. As a result, I did not even *visit* the country of my birth for the next twenty years. I got a very good job in London, becoming a medical consultant. Having specialized in neuroscience, in 1979 I was appointed to a chair of neuropathology (the study of the nervous system: brain, spinal cord, nerves and muscles) at King's College London.

Ilona (Ili), my mother

Me and my mother, after the war.

Less than a year after we had returned, my mother and Uncle
Jenő were successfully running the timber yard – while they
could. Soon after the Communists' takeover, large private
enterprises were closed down or nationalized – that is, taken
over by the state. With heavy hearts, Mum and Uncle Jenő
had to close the timber yard in 1949.

With her share of the money raised, my mother purchased some gold jewellery. In fact, it was the capital which paid for my university education. Pieces were sold as and when we needed money.

Me and my mother, around 1955.

Fortunately, Mum found work as an accountant at the local branch of the National Bank. However, this did not last long. As a member of a "capitalist" family, she was soon sacked.

My mother was not easily defeated. She got a job as a cashier in a large state-owned food store in the main square in town. By 1950 food was scarce, choice minimal and half of the shelves empty. It was a depressing place to work. Later she got a better job in a men's fashion shop.

When she retired, she came to live with me, and we moved into a flat in a modern block in Szeged in November 1967. She died in February 1968 in a street accident.

My mother, later in life

Mum never talked about the deportation or Bergen-Belsen. Not until, as a teenager, I started to ask questions. She had struggled to regain her religious beliefs and make peace with the fate of so many in our family.

There was, above all, one wound which never healed: that caused by the death of my brother. She mourned him until the very end of her life.

My brother, Gyuri.

Uncle Jenő

When the timber yard closed down, like my mother, Uncle Jenő found himself without a job. However, he was soon employed by a nationalized company producing building materials. But, once again, this did not last long.

My uncle, Jenö.

He joined, as an accountant, a so-called co-operative firm, composed of craftsmen who voluntarily joined and were relatively independent. It produced household goods and he worked there until his retirement. He visited me a couple of times in London and died in 1986 of a heart attack in the restaurant of a hotel in Makó.

Uncle Jenö and two Russian soldiers, late 1945 or early 1946.

Grandma

My cousin, Magda, my grandmother and grandfather, my cousin, Pista (front, left), who was killed in Auschwitz and my brother, Gyuri (front, right), in around 1932 or earlier.

Sixty years later, I tried to find information about Grandma's death in Austria, without any success. I searched archives in Vienna and Wiener Neustadt and met historians and eye-witnesses, but could not find any trace of her existence or death.

Aunt Anna and Zsuzsi

As we learned after we had returned home, Aunt Anna and Zsuzsi's train had transported them to Auschwitz, where they must have been gassed on arrival. They shared their terrible deaths with more than 500,000 Hungarian Jews who were all killed in Auschwitz and elsewhere during the summer of 1944.

No known photos of Aunt Anna and Zsuzsi survive.

Aunt Márta and Uncle Lajos

As a teenager, I spent one month of my summer holidays with Aunt Márta and Uncle Lajos. They were heartbroken when I decided to remain in England in 1969. I felt guilty for having let them down. We wrote to each other regularly and several times a year I would send parcels – containing chiefly fashion items that were difficult or expensive to get at the time in Hungary. Both died in the 1980s.

Me, my aunt, Márta, my uncle, Lajos, and my mother in around 1953.

George Gross
(The unnamed American officer)

Our liberation by the Americans on 13 April 1945 was an unforgettable day. I have always remembered the first American officer who took our pictures. When I started to research the past, I decided to try to find him.

After a great deal of research, one day a long letter arrived. It was from George Gross, the American tank commander who had liberated us. We started to correspond, and in his second letter several photographs arrived, including one with a group of children. After looking at it under a magnifying glass, I concluded that one of the boys must have been me. I visited him in San Diego in America, where he lived with his family as a retired professor of English at the University of California San Diego. We became friends and regularly kept in touch until his death in 2009.

He was kind enough to share the following photos with me

George Gross, with his tank, one month before liberation.

Gina Rappaport, who translated for the prisoners being liberated from the train.

A German soldier, surrendering.

A group of liberated prisoners, i

A group of liberated prisoners, ii

A group of liberated prisoners, iii

A group of liberated prisoners, iv

About the places on my journey

See maps on pages 202 to 205

Makó

A small town in the south-eastern corner of Hungary. In 1920 its population was 37,000, with the Jewish community numbering 2,380 or 6.45 per cent. One hundred years later, in 2019, only 22,390 people lived there, and the number of Jews was reduced to as few as ten.

The synagogue of which my family were members was consecrated in 1914 and demolished in 1965, despite having been one of the most beautiful landmarks in town. The schools where I was a pupil, my birthplace, my grandparents' house and the two villas of my uncles, despite changes during the years, have all survived.

Szeged

A major provincial centre in south-eastern Hungary. With a population of 175,000 it is Hungary's third largest city. In 1941, 4,161 Jews lived there; sixty years later, in 2001, this number was reduced to 184.

There is a memorial of our deportation in front of the brick factory in which we stayed in June 1944.

Strasshof

A small town with a population today of just over 10,000 (as of 2018). It lies about thirty kilometres east of Vienna. Many of the trains carrying Jews from Hungary arrived in this town, which had a busy railway yard.

Wiener Neustadt

This small city of 44,820 people (as of 2018) is some fifty kilometres south of Vienna. When I visited Wiener Neustadt sixty years later, I saw a very pretty city with beautiful old buildings, restored after the war.

Bergen-Belsen

Inmates of the camp with members of the British army after liberation

Bergen-Belsen was one of the most notorious concentration camps in an enormous network which Nazi Germany established before and during the Second World War. The history of this camp goes back before the war, when some thirty barracks were erected to house German and Polish workers condemned for hard labour. With the outbreak of war, it became a camp for prisoners of war – first for French and Belgian soldiers, later for Russians.

It was transformed into a concentration camp in 1943 and the same year declared a special camp. Its main aim was to hold Jewish people as prisoners potentially to be exchanged for German citizens who had been stranded in enemy (that is, Allied) countries, or later for goods, like trucks, medicines and food. For this reason, in principle, we should have been kept alive. Why then did prisoners die by the thousands? The camp was originally designed to hold 5,000–6,000 prisoners. In the end there were ten times more. The numbers were swelled by prisoners transferred from camps in the east, before the Russian Army could liberate them.

In the grossly overcrowded camps, epidemics broke out which killed many people. Prisoners also died of starvation. This is why the liberating British Army found, on 15 April 1945, a "hell on earth": unburied corpses lying by the hundreds on the ground and in the barracks. The British soldiers, ancillary workers and medical staff performed miracles to provide food, water and medication. They also ordered the Nazi guards to bury the corpses in mass graves. In one of these lies my father. German civilian leaders had to witness the scene: to see the crimes committed in their name.

Despite all the horrors of Bergen-Belsen, it was not a general policy to tattoo the prisoners with their numbers. Neither my parents nor I had such an identification. I learned our numbers from the camp's records.

British soldiers burning down the camp's barracks

On 21 May 1945, after the last prisoners were transferred to safety, the British Army burned down all the barracks. When I visited Bergen-Belsen for the first time as a British citizen, in 1973, I was disappointed, since there were no obvious remnants of the camps, apart from some foundations of the barracks. There were mass graves with the approximate numbers of dead on the tombstones: 5,000, 1,000, and many other rounded-up numbers. And there was an impressive memorial.

The Bergen-Belsen memorial

Every year, on my birthday, I receive a card from Bergen-Belsen. It is a heart-warming gesture, although I think I am even happier than my German friends are that I had survived.

Farsleben

It was outside this small German village that the train, carrying us from Bergen-Belsen to Theresienstadt, was liberated by the Americans. It has a population of only 920 and lies 165 kilometres from Bergen-Belsen.

Prisoners freed by members of the 743rd Tank Battalion, 13 April 1945

Hillersleben

Hillersleben is a small, prosperous village of under 900 people.

Separated by a motorway lies the estate, built for German officers, in which we stayed after liberation in 1945. Since this area was within the boundary of the Russian Zone of Occupation, the Red Army made their home there until all the Russian soldiers left Germany in 1994.

When I visited in 2003 for the first time since I'd stayed there as a child, the place was completely deserted. The once-attractive houses were decaying, and weeds were growing everywhere. Later, bulldozers arrived and demolished all the buildings, and now it is a field of solar panels. This undoubtedly serves a useful purpose, but the evidence of a chapter of our journey has vanished for ever.

Prague

We only travelled across this city and changed trains at one of the stations. At the time, it was the capital of Czechoslovakia, now the Czech Republic. I visited Prague and had correspondence with the National Archives. The information they gave was general, mainly concerning the enormous number of people who travelled across the city at the end of the Second World War. Of course, finding anything about us was even less likely than finding a needle in a haystack.

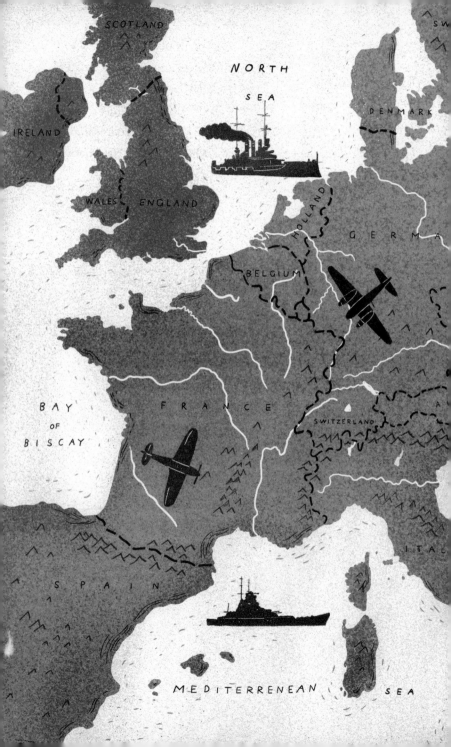

Europe in 1944

At the beginning of 1944, Belgium, Holland, Denmark, Norway, Austria, Poland and parts of France, the Soviet Union and Czechoslovakia were under occupation by Nazi Germany.

DENMARK

HOLLAND

Bergen-Belsen

Farsleben

Magdeburg

GERMANY

BELGIU

Prague

CZE

Cattle wagon from Strasshof
to Bergen-Belsen

Wiene

FRANCE

AUSTRI

Wiener Neustadt

ITALY

Peter's Journey

EAST PRUSSIA

P O L A N D

U S S R

Bergen-Belsen

Makó: Timber yard

OSLOVANIA

Strasshof

eustadt · Budapest

HUNGARY

R U M A N I A

Szeged · Makó

BULGARIA

Szeged University

Glossary

Air raid

An attack by military planes on a surface target.

Baccalaureate

The final set of examinations at the end of the last (fourth) year of high school, around the age of eighteen. It is popular in several European countries, particularly in France. At the time when I was in high school there were four to five compulsory subjects like literature, history, physics and mathematics.

Barracks

Buildings used to house special groups of people, such as soldiers, prisoners or labourers, in a simple or even primitive environment.

Barbed wire

Steel wire with sharp points at regular intervals. It is used for fencing. In Bergen-Belsen there was electricity running through it.

Cantor
A religious official of a synagogue who conducts part of the service, singing or chanting the prayers.

Casino
A public building or room, reserved for social occasions, usually for gambling.

Communism
An extreme left-wing system of ideas. It advocates a classless society in which everybody is equal and aims to replace private property with public ownership.

Cooling tower
A structure which decreases the temperature of hot water, chiefly by evaporation.

Crematorium
A building in which the bodies of the dead are burned (cremated).

Deportation
The transportation of people against their will, usually to unknown destinations.

Dictatorship
An oppressive form of government in which one person (the dictator) or a small group of people exercises absolute power.

Dysentery
A disease affecting digestion caused by bacteria. The main symptoms are bloody diarrhoea, tummy pain and a high temperature.

Fascism
Fascism is an extreme right-wing political ideology and mass movement. It is characterized by aggressive nationalism and disapproval of democracy. When in power, fascists suppress opposition. Their leader usually becomes a dictator (*see above*).

In Germany, the National Socialist (Nazi) Party came to power in 1933 with its leader, Adolf Hitler, becoming head of government. In Hungary, the Arrow Cross Party was a fascist party in power for a short time between October 1944 and April 1945.

Garrison

A group or unit of troops stationed in a fortress or town.

Gendarmes

In Hungary before the Second World War there were two forces maintaining law and order: policemen and gendarmes. While their roles overlapped, their uniforms and chains of command were different. The gendarmes were active mainly in the countryside. Their role did not finish with maintaining order, they also had a political function: to support the government of the day – if necessary, by the use of force.

Gothic typeface

A type of font that was popular in early printed books from the fifteenth and sixteenth century and is in used in modern Germany. In the UK it is not used often. A couple of the best-known examples are the mastheads of the *Daily Telegraph* (UK) and the *New York Times* (USA) newspapers.

Jeep

A well-built, powerful motor vehicle with four-wheel drive designed chiefly for military use. The word comes from the American army slang of 1940 for the military term "general purpose" vehicle, or "GP".

Kosher

This word is used to describe food which conforms to strict Jewish religious laws. There are many rules, but three of the best known are: it is forbidden to eat pork, or any food prepared from pigs, it is forbidden to mix meat and milk products, and it is forbidden to eat shellfish.

Latrine

A latrine is a communal toilet, usually found in camps and barracks. Its simplest form is a trench dug in the earth. This is what the latrine was like in Bergen-Belsen.

Malnutrition

Poor nutrition, when the body does not get the right amount and type of food, resulting in unintentional weight loss. Malnourished people feel weak and tired most of the time and have reduced resistance to infections. Children suffering from malnutrition may not grow at the expected rate.

Red Army

The Red Army was the army of the Soviet Union, created by the Communist Party in 1918. This name was abandoned in 1946.

Star of David

A generally recognized sign of Jewish identity and Judaism, the Jewish religion. It has the same level of significance for Jews as the cross for Christians and the star and crescent for Muslims.

Torah

The Torah is the central and most important document of the Jewish religion. The word "Torah" means to guide or to teach. It is composed of the first five books of the Hebrew Bible. It also forms part, in the form of the Old Testament, of the Christian Bible.

Typhoid fever

This disease, caused by bacteria, can affect many organs of the body. Patients suffer from fever, headache, constipation and coughs. Later tummy ache and diarrhoea can develop.

Typhus

Typhus is an infectious disease caused by bacteria, which are spread by lice, fleas and mites. It is characterized by high fever, headache, diarrhoea, feeling sick, dry cough, joint ____ ____ically spotty rash, appearing first on the chest, ____ spread all over the body.

Water closet (WC)

A lavatory (toilet) in which human waste is flushed down by water. Its abbreviated form, WC, is more often used to mark public conveniences in mainland Europe than in the UK.

ACKNOWLEDGMENTS

I wish to thank Elspeth Sinclair, who edited my manuscript with patience and care; Emily Hibbs, who put the manuscript into its final shape for Scholastic; Philip Parker for his attentive read-through; Matthew Grundy Haigh for his meticulous review; Sarah Baldwin for her design expertise; Hannah Love for her publicity support; Georgi Russell for her production know-how; Victoria Stebleva for her cover illustrations and maps. The encouragement of Elizabeth Scoggins of Scholastic has been greatly appreciated.

Thanks is due, too, to Judge Jeremy Connor and Richard Bates for their advice during the preparation of the manuscript. I am grateful to Emma Matthewson for helping me find the right publisher for my book.